ABIGAIL MOOR:
THE DARKEST DAWN

Miss Abigail Hammond grows up in Beckton Manor as the adopted daughter of Lord Hammond. However, when he falls terminally ill, her life, her identity and her safety are all threatened. Then, faced with being forced into a marriage to a man she loathes, she runs away with her maid on Lord Hammond's instructions. Abigail tries to discover the truth of her past, despite her efforts being constantly foiled by her life-long maid, Martha.

VALERIE HOLMES

ABIGAIL MOOR: THE DARKEST DAWN

Complete and Unabridged

LINFORD
Leicester

First published in Great Britain in 2011

First Linford Edition
published 2011

British Library CIP Data

Holmes, Valerie.
　Abigail Moor: the darkest dawn. - -
(Linford romance library)
　1. Adoptees- -Fiction. 2. Nobility- -Fiction.
　3. Forced marriage- -Fiction. 4. Love stories.
　5. Large type books.
　I. Title II. Series
　823.9′2–dc22

ISBN 978–1–4448–0688–5

Published by
F. A. Thorpe (Publishing)
Anstey, Leicestershire

Set by Words & Graphics Ltd.
Anstey, Leicestershire
Printed and bound in Great Britain by
T. J. International Ltd., Padstow, Cornwall

This book is printed on acid-free paper

1

Abigail looked him straight in the eye. He was her brother's manservant and therefore should be obeying her. Standing opposite him, wearing her delicate white muslin gown, which unfortunately served only to accentuate the flushed pink of her cheeks, she tried one final time to make him bend to her will instead of upholding his master's.

'I wish to see my father.' Abigail picked nervously at the fine embroidery on her sleeve. The high-waisted dress was one of her prettiest and she knew it suited her slender figure. She had hoped that Frederick's manservant would be touched by her predicament and let her inside the room — just for a few precious moments.

'I'm sorry, Miss Hammond, but Lord Hammond is not to be disturbed. I have been given my orders.' He bowed his head slightly, apologetically in manner even, but his eyes never blinked as they stared defiantly back at hers. Abigail knew she had not melted his hard heart, nor even begun to prickle his conscience. He stood a head and shoulders higher than her. She found him intimidating which only served to annoy Abigail further. She was his better. Abigail held her head high, her pride dented. How could he have been given authority over her, in her own home? The situation was becoming intolerable.

'Then please go and inform Mr Frederick that I have no appetite today and shall not be taking dinner with him tonight.' Abigail glared at him, challenging him to defy her second command.

He glanced at the locked bedchamber door and, thankfully, Abigail thought, decided it was safe to leave his post for the few moments it would take to deliver her message downstairs where her brother lounged in her father's library.

Abigail smiled fleetingly as she watched him walk down the long carpeted corridor. He was, she mused, dressed in the livery of a fool. She bent down and reached behind the chair that the manservant, Simpson, had been standing next to. Her father always kept a spare key there in case he forgot his own. Lord Hammond was a private man, who took care to keep the doors to his personal room locked to any but his most trusted servant. She was about to turn that key in the lock when she heard Frederick and his man talking on the stairs. Abigail opened the door opposite and hid for a few moments, leaving the tiniest of gaps between the door and the surround to peep through. She was breathing deeply, but tried to still herself.

'Go to the kitchens now, whilst I speak to Lord Hammond! Next time, do not dare to leave your post unless 'I' have ordered it!' He was shouting at the man, yet he was no more than one foot away from him.

Abigail saw the manservant bow low, his fist clenched at his side, before he walked away. No wonder he had not given in to her gentle appeal; her brother was showing a much sterner side to his nature than she had previously seen.

Frederick entered her father's room. Once inside, she crept across the landing and listened silently by the door.

'Father, I am glad to see you are looking somewhat better. Do you still take Dr Pinkerton's medication? I travelled up from York as soon as I received word of your situation.' Frederick's voice was always clear. As a senior partner in his own law firm, he delivered his words to create an effect. His confident manner had impressed Abigail, until yesterday when he had returned to Beckton Manor. He had set off as soon as Abigail's letter had arrived informing him of his father's deterioration. With Lord Hammond ill abed, his attitude towards her had become distant. At eleven years her senior she had always respected him as her brother.

Abigail could not hear Lord Hammond's reply. His voice was too weak and low.

'Good. Now that I am here, you have no need to worry about a thing . . . '

There was a pause, then Frederick laughed, but it held no humour. 'My dear Father, your concerns are oh so predictable. Always Abigail, isn't it? What of her future? I believe I have told you before that the one mistake people make in this life, is regarding their final arrangements and yet you are no exception. If only you had listened to my advice — but then, when have you ever? People think themselves inde-structible, leaving until tomorrow what they should have done yesterday. So, now you are reaching your time of few tomorrows and you have left issues undone and words unsaid.'

There was a moment of relative quiet, whilst her father answered.

'No, don't upset yourself, sir. I have had a lifetime to adjust to it, and to patiently prepare for such a time. Fret not, for Frederick's future, Father, is quite safe. I am your son and heir and I shall claim my birthright. Do not worry yourself about your dear Abigail. I shall see she is suitably matched to your business friend Mr Jeremy Hackman. He will give her all that she needs and she will give him what he needs — or else he will enjoy taking it.'

He laughed and Abigail felt a shiver run through her body. A match to a total stranger!

'Now if you'll excuse me. Your tray will be brought to you soon.'

Abigail ran back inside the room opposite as Frederick left, locking the door behind him.

Once he had walked away, she slowly turned the spare key to release the handle before Simpson repositioned himself outside. Inside the room she tiptoed over to where the figure of Lord Hammond lay motionless in the bed.

Abigail's chest tightened, she felt cold, fear grew that he might have already slipped away from this world, after the harshness of Frederick's outburst.

'I wondered how long it would be before you found your way to me.' His voice was low and hoarse. 'You will have to be brave, dear Abigail. Now Frederick is here, and my worst fears have been confirmed, you shall have to leave. I'm sorry, I . . .'

'Father, Frederick is here to take care of things.' An invisible lump caught in her throat. 'Father, are you . . . ? Will you . . . ? Frederick will send for the best of doctors . . .' Abigail blustered. 'Why do I have to marry this man?' She squeezed his hand gently.

'If you are asking me if I am very ill, then I should have to answer-yes.' He coughed and swallowed with some difficulty. 'Abigail, I shall die, as we all must, but when I do not know. No one does.'

He sighed heavily and Abigail could see for herself how tired he was, as if her eyes had been forced to acknowledge what they had not previously wanted to see.

Abigail could not come to terms with

7

either her father's situation or her own. Life had always been so simple — straightforward. Now, everything precious to her was under threat.

'My beautiful Abigail, there is so much I should have told you. How blind I have been. I thought Frederick would look after you, but I have seen him in his true light, for he has shown his bitterness to me. I have been blinkered by my own love for him. I have let him down in some way. Forgive an old fool his folly.' He coughed and Abigail looked to the door nervously in case Frederick's servant should enter. 'You must be strong. You must leave us. Take your maid, Martha, with you for she knows something of where you came from and it is time you were told the truth.'

'Father, I cannot leave you. You are ill and I have no money of my own. What would I do and where would I go? Why should I have to?' Abigail pleaded.

'Frederick is jealous of you. He would marry you off to a man I would not give a dog to! Mr Jeremy Hackman is a hard man, wealthy, and gaining more money as his mills take up more land. He is not for you. Listen, child, you will go to my study,' his voice was heavy with emotion and breaking as he spoke to her, 'Remove the Bible from the shelf to the left of the window. It is a false book — no not the Bible itself,' he added, as he saw the shock on Abigail's face. 'The Lord has been protecting some treasured secrets for me these last few years. Take it. Go to York. Martha will keep you safe, and then follow the instructions inside the letter.' He stopped to catch his breath and closed his eyes.

'Father, please say I can fetch Reverend Hardiman.'

'No! I'm in no state for that, and Frederick is not my enemy. He may be yours, but he is still my son and my heir. I must try to be strong so that I can put right the wrong I have done to my two children in different ways. He is angry with me, not evil, Abigail. This is family business and nothing to do with anyone else. Take the money from my bottom drawer in that cabinet over there and go tonight. Think not of me, but of yourself.' He fell silent once more.

She kissed his cheek and held his cold hand. 'I cannot leave you, Father . . . ' His skin was clammy, his nightshirt soaked and she wanted to call the maid and have them change him and his bedding again. But she realised she had to leave quickly before she was found there. She wished she had delayed sending word, but then if anything happened to him, Frederick would have been rightly furious with her.

'Obey me, this once, child, for I shall not be able to watch over you if you stay here. I gave you a chance to have a good life, but absently I did not safeguard your future as well as I hid your past.'

As his breathing became shallower, Abigail flushed with emotion. 'Hid what of my past? I don't understand.'

'You must leave . . . ' He did not

open his eyes again, but Abigail saw the moisture of tears seep from his closed lids. 'Look after yourself, Abigail, unless you wish to obey your brother's wishes.'

Abigail removed the money from the drawer. She gasped at the amount. 'Father, there is so much.'

'Take it all with my blessing and be safe and happy again. Go to Mr Joseph Ashton, of *Scrimshaw, Bushy and Ashton* in York, and arrange for him to come here forthwith with a good and trusted doctor, as I would like to try to correct my mistake with legal represen-tation . . . using a person who has no blood relationship to me. I will try to put my affairs in order before it is too late. Do this, and leave Frederick to me. I have created such bitterness in him. Now go, I beg of you.'

Abigail swallowed hard, 'What has been hidden about my past?'

He did not answer her. She kissed his cheek then left to return the key to its hiding place and quietly entered her own room.

She wasted no time in hiding the money and made straight for her father's study. It seemed strange entering the room without him being seated behind his desk or sitting in his chair by the fireside. It was as if the room had lost its soul — just books and ledgers. She reached up for the Bible as she had been instructed to and, hugging it closely to her, made her way across the hallway. She intended to return unnoticed to her room so that Martha could pack a few belongings for her. It made no sense to her. Why should she have to leave her home, the lovely Beckton Manor, in such a clandestine way? However, her father was adamant and she was scared. Abigail took comfort thinking Martha would know what to do; she always did.

'Abigail, my dear, you are feeling better I see. Perhaps you will now join us for our meal.' Frederick's voice surprised her and she nearly dropped the book on the main staircase.

'What do you have there, that you

would cling to so desperately?'

'I'm afraid I still feel unwell, that is why I sought solace in Father's Bible.' Abigail looked around. 'What do you mean, 'us'?'

A stout figure appeared in the doorway of the drawing room. Abigail shivered involuntarily. He smiled broadly at her and bowed low.

'It is with great pleasure that I make your acquaintance, Miss Hammond, and equal sadness because we have not met under happier circumstances than your poor father's ill health.'

Abigail looked directly at the man's chubby features. There was something about his eyes that made her feel ill at ease, no matter what honeyed words slipped off his tongue.

'I thank you for your concern, sir. If you will excuse me, I have much to ask our Lord. I am sure Father will return to full health once more.'

'Of course, it is right that you should believe that. Anything less would never do.' Frederick gestured with his hand, she breathed deeply, relieved that she was being dismissed. 'Then, when you have finished your devotions, you can thank the good Lord that this very day your prayers have been answered,' he added.

'How so?' Abigail turned around to face him.

'I have found you the perfect suitor, and he is most anxious to meet you properly. He is a man of maturity, means and ambition, indeed a man after my own heart.' He looked at the man next to him. 'Mr Jeremy Hackman. Your future is secure, as I promised you it would be.' Both men grinned broadly at her openly shocked expression.

Abigail felt as though she was frozen in time. Her feet were rooted to the stair on which she stood as she looked from her brother's deep brown eyes to Mr Hackman's pock-marked features and balding head.

'I could not possibly even think of such a thing when my father lies ill abed,' Abigail protested.

'Oh, but you can. You see, it will be a

small ceremony in the family chapel of course and soon, very soon, because of Father's declining health. All is arranged, my dear Abigail. Do not worry yourself, for everything has been planned in great detail.'

With no reply possible she silently ran back up the stairs as the two men entered the drawing room, obviously in high spirits.

★ ★ ★

Placing a chair against the bedchamber door, she carefully rested the Bible on the bed cover. She wanted to know what was hidden inside this holy book, but she had to act quickly, to save her father and herself from Frederick's clutches. But how could she without being discovered? She opened her dressing room door and to her horror saw that her travelling clothes and her best boots had been removed; so, too, had her small valise.

Shocked, she stepped backwards.

Well, if he had pre-empted her intentions then she would have to travel as a servant! Abigail had the money her father had given her. When she arrived at York she would go to a ladies' outfitter and make arrangements for new attire. Fleetingly the thought of spending money for herself appealed to her. Quickly she hid the money on her person and held the Bible closely to her. Some of the pages were still whole, but there was a hollow in the middle where three sealed letters had been carefully folded in place.

Was it a sin to cut the Bible in such a way? Surely not, she reasoned. After all, her father was a noble and a God-fearing man. She shook her head dismissing the notion that the current illness that had befallen him had something to do with the act of sacrilege. She must know who they were for and what secrets they held.

A knock was heard at the door.

Quickly, she closed the book concealing the letters. Her curiosity would have to wait to be sated.

'Who is it?' Abigail tried to keep her voice level, aware that Simpson was still on duty outside her father's bedroom.

'It's Martha, Miss Hammond, with your tray.' Martha's voice was more polite than her usually familiar manner, which told Abigail straight away that Simpson was watching her.

Abigail allowed Martha to step inside. She placed the tray down on a table and lifted off the linen napkin that covered it.

'Martha, he has removed my travel clothes and . . . '

'No, miss, I did.' Martha's cheeks were flushed with emotion.

Abigail realised she must have been very upset by the day's events. This had been her home, too. Her anger at Frederick grew, replacing fear with a determination to thwart his vile intentions. Martha, too, was being forced to leave as Abigail herself was, and both deeply resented it.

'What do you know, Martha? How

do you know it? Have you spoken to Father?' Abigail's mind was filled with unanswered questions. Namely, what secrets had Lord Hammond kept from her?

Abigail sipped the green tea that Martha had prepared for her; she was in great need of the warm liquid as it soothed her dry throat.

'I took in his tray. There are things I need to tell you but not now! We have to get you away. It may not be easy,' Martha glanced at the door, 'You are watched.' Martha removed the Bible from the bed where Abigail had rested it. She turned back the sheets.

'What are you doing, Martha? I am not a child and this is no time to go to bed!' Abigail spoke sharply and was surprised by the very terse reply she received.

'It is precisely the time to go to bed! You are upset, weak — a female, the anxiety has given you a head that aches; it could develop into an ague should you not rest. Climb in.'

Abigail was about to put up a fight when she heard voices. Frederick was talking to his man. Worse, his footsteps were coming towards her door.

Martha pointed to the bed. 'Remember when as a child you would do anything to get to Cook's cakes when there was a function at the manor and you had been sent to bed?'

'Of course, Martha, but . . . '

'Tonight, I'll be in the kitchens.' Her voice was hardly audible, but Abigail nodded agreement. Questions would have to wait till later.

Abigail lay in between the sheets and let her hair fall freely about her shoulders as if she was retiring. Martha put the lace bonnet upon Abigail's head as she had done so many times before, and sat on the side of the bed holding the Bible on her lap.

Abigail looked at it, eyes wide, when the door opened. She had no time to warn Martha, but prayed that the letters inside were not discovered.

'Miss Abigail is feeling unwell, Mr

Hammond. Her head ... it aches badly.' Martha tried to sound humble, but Abigail knew that her maid would love to take a hand to Frederick as she had cuffed him once as a boy. The boy, now the man, had never forgotten the experience and he was showing that he had never forgiven her either.

'How very predictable, Abigail. Your world has changed, so you've taken to your bed.' He paused and grabbed the Bible from Martha's hand, Abigail let out a small gasp, as he unceremoniously flipped it onto the tray. 'That book will not protect you, nor your 'ex' maid.' He glared at Martha as she scurried over to the tray.

With the maid's back to him Abigail could see that Martha was busily covering the tray with the napkin, carefully slipping one of the letters back within its pages.

'Ex-maid?' Abigail repeated, taking his attention away from Martha who left the room carrying the tray.

'Yes, you shall be part of a new

household. We have found her a more suitable position — in the Asylum, helping those moderately less fortunate than herself. Mr Hackman is one of their generous benefactors. You shall have a more able and suitable maid, befitting your new lifestyle as a 'lady' of position in York.'

'The asylum! When . . . will this happen?'

'Soon, my dear Abigail . . . oh so soon.'

2

Joshua Rusk left the inn with bleary eyes and a tired body. He stretched to his full height and stared at a cobalt sky. It would be a long journey to London but better to go than stay. He ached and rubbed his leg. The bullet had gone, the scar and the aches remained, but he would be fit again, and soon. He had left good men still fighting in the war and he felt for them. Part of him wanted to return, to warn them of the bleak future they faced at home, jobless, penniless and hungry. But then, if he did, what fire would that put in their bellies to fight for their country. Their own Regent might have sadly let them down, but Napoleon would offer nothing but death to their kith and kin should he successfully invade. 'Choices,' he mused, the world was full of them.

He placed his high hat upon his head

and buttoned up his caped travelling cloak and stood patiently as the ostler made the coach ready. His bag was tossed aloft and tethered. York would be the first stop. He waited whilst a lady and her husband climbed in, then a captain of the Militia, and lastly, a man of fashion. He toyed with the idea of riding atop, but his ticket was for inside. So he removed his hat, unbuttoned his coat and took his seat. He rested his leg against the side of the coach as he squeezed in next to the married couple. The husband took more than his share of the seat but as Joshua stared out as the coach began its journey, he settled as he had suffered far more uncomfortable situations with his men than this one. He closed his eyes to the world and remembered the skirmishes fought, men lost and battles won. One day he would be free of the memories and the pain, but not the scars. Until then, he opened his eyes once more and marvelled at the dramatic shadows which played around on the moorland scenery. Such was life — one minute full of colour shape and beauty, the next dark, menacing and gloomy. The memory of Francesca's face pained him more than his wound. Her lovely life, her beauty, her last breath . . . he could not save her. There had been no qualified surgeons to treat her in the village, unlike his own wound, which had been treated by the best Edinburgh had produced. Pain . . . his leg and heart held too much of it. He would return to London, remain a bachelor, and when he was fully fit once more, he would embark to a whole new world.

★ ★ ★

Abigail stared at Frederick, his dark figure standing awkwardly at the foot of her bed. 'You've changed so.' She tried to sound confident rather than vulnerable. 'I don't understand why you are so angry with me. Is it something I've done, Frederick?' Abigail wanted to try

24

to reach out to him, give him one last chance to explain why he was being so hard and totally unyielding. There was no reason why her life should change from what it always had been, if he willed it so.

'You are not of our family. In fact, you are a penniless orphan who has no rights as a female; you are a bastard — a child born to a Jezebel!'

He folded his arms across the immaculately buttoned up coat, peering down at her, his sinewy figure accentuated by the black trousers and tail coat that he was accustomed to wearing. She recoiled, holding the bed cover close to her. She had never been spoken to in such a way. Her father had rescued her from an alms house, and Martha, her maid, had been hired to tend her, as she did to this very day.

'Do not look so aggrieved, Abigail. You have shared my home and my father's affection for these last twenty years. I have found your presence tolerable as your frivolous and childlike countenance has pleased Father immensely.'

'How can you say such things? Have you not been and are you not still my brother in every right but by blood? An accident of birth created me, but God placed me in your father's arms . . . as his child. How can you turn on me now he is so ill?' She was almost pleading with him to see reason, but he stood there behind his cool façade and stared back silently at her for a moment.

'It is your naivety that is your most appealing grace and folly in equal measure. Blood, my girl, is everything to everyone who has good blood running through their veins; it goes along with money and position. You have no blood to be proud of. Beyond our generosity you have no wealth.' He raised his arms as if encompassing everything around them. 'This leaves only position. You have been allowed to have one whilst you have lived at Beckton Manor. However, you must realise that if you were to come out, with the other girls, you would be the joke of society; considered no more than a weed amongst prime roses in full bloom. No, Abigail, your position is both unenviable and untenable. It is a matter to which I have given a deal of thought over the last few years.'

Abigail had never felt so threatened, trapped by Frederick's words and manner. He was not the person she had thought him to be. Her father was right . . . Lord Edmond Hammond, the only father she had ever known . . . she would have to escape.

Underneath the hurt and humiliation another emotion was stirring within her — rage. How dare he presume to talk to her so? Her future could be as pleasant or hard as he chose to make it. There, Abigail knew, lay the problem, her destiny was at the mercy of his will — his will, unfortunately, declared she become his puppet, to obey him and serve his ends in life.

He continued, 'I have decided you will be best suited to a man with new money who needs a young wife to breed, who knows how to behave and give his success respectability . . . '

'An old man with new money,' she added bitterly.

'Beggars, my girl, cannot be choosers. He has no fine blood either, although his parents were married. His mills and the asylum have earned a decent position, along with his natural business acumen for seeing an opportunity and taking it. Yes, he is a sound match for a favoured companion of Lord Hammond; you shall make him an obedient and pliant wife and a very happy man. That is my decision, so dress yourself and join both of us for dinner as it would be in your best interest not to vex your future husband unnecessarily. I am told he is of a most pleasant temperament, unless crossed.'

He smiled at her and bowed slightly, mockingly, before leaving the room. Abigail leaped from the bed as soon as the door was shut.

'Damn you to hell and back Frederick Hammond! I will not dance to your tune!' Abigail snapped as she gathered her thoughts together. She opened her window. The steep drop beneath the ledge somehow seemed far greater than it had when she was just a young child. She would have presumed the opposite would be the case. Strange how, as a girl, she had risked life and limb and never given her antics a moment's thought for her own safety. Escaping from her room had been an adventure and worth Cook's rebuke to gain a glass of warmed, honeyed milk and her freshly baked parkin by the open kitchen fire, before being smuggled back to her bedchamber. Martha would then tuck her in and stay with her until she went soundly to sleep. It had all seemed normal and right, but as she viewed it now, she realised it was a pampered existence, one she had apparently no right to.

Yet, here, standing in her dress, she realised that the second she committed herself to this act of escapology, she would say goodbye to everything and everyone that had ever meant anything to her within her twenty years of life, except Martha who would be leaving with her. Never before had she had to literally step out in pure faith. A picture of the man, Hackman, formed in her mind, of being married to such a man, and shamelessly she thought of the long intimate nights that would lie heavily ahead of them. Abigail felt nauseous at the thought of the man's stubby fingers touching her body, and took a deep breath. 'Now or never!' She placed her foot precariously onto the narrow ledge. She clung to the building; the cold air seemed almost to pinch her skin. Far from being scared, though, a different sensation filled her — an old, almost unfamiliar feeling, the excitement of her adventure. She inched around the corner of the hall leaving her window behind, placing her foot onto the top of a gargoyle's head. It peered out into the night almost unnoticed from the ground, yet it was such a striking carving. She moved swiftly across the length of the lower roof like a fairy of the night, her steps soundless.

When she had reached the southern hall, she was above the servants' quarters. Now all she had to do was climb down the drainage pipe. This, Abigail discovered, was a far greater obstacle when one was full-grown and wearing a dress. When she was but five feet from the ground the old metal bracket parted from the wall. She clung on tightly to the pipe as it came away. Abigail curled into a ball and, despite the urge to scream, let the force take her backwards into three successive rolls before she stopped, spread-eagled on the cobbled yard. This was not the start to her adventure she had hoped for, exposed to the bitter cold, dirt and damp air.

'Miss Abigail, child! This is no time to be playing silly games.' Martha's harsh rebuke was said accusingly in a clear whisper.

It nearly caused Abigail to shout out

in denial and indignation — as if she would dream of doing such a thing under the circumstances! She quickly stood up, slightly bruised and muddied. However, both women ran for the kitchen door, from behind which the light of a lantern flickered. Cook hugged Abigail firmly, all of a fluster and at a loss for words. Unceremoniously she was bundled with Martha into the dairy rooms. Her clothes were revealed from where they had been hidden under a large piece of muslin and her bag behind the large milk churns.

'Hurry, Miss Abigail, please change quickly.' Cook pointed to the clothes.

'It's freezing in here!' Abigail protested, but started to undress when she saw the stern look on Martha's face.

'Soon as you're gone I'll put your gown in the laundry; that'll hide any evidence of your being here.' Mrs Grimes nodded in agreement with herself, as was her habit. No sooner was the dress off Abigail's back than she bustled away with it.

Martha shook her head. 'She's broken hearted, Miss Abigail. She loves you so much. I pray we may safely return one day . . . soon.' Martha watched as Abigail laced up her boots.

'What did you do with the Bible, Martha?' Abigail looked at her maid, whose behaviour appeared to be changing more determinedly each minute.

'It's in here.' Martha picked up the bag.

'What do you know about it, Martha?' Abigail asked, as she took the heavy leather travel bag from her servant, then realised its true weight.

Martha, with a firm, sturdy grip, took it back. 'It's the 'Good Book'. Now, let's have less chatter.'

'Where is the carriage?' Abigail asked, and was surprised when Martha turned around almost laughing in her face.

'Lord preserve us! This is not going to be easy, is it, lass? Common sense should tell you there isn't one.' Martha shook her head.

Abigail stared at her, indignantly. She was going to rebuke her maid.

'Should we summon all the servants in the house or perhaps ask Mr Frederick Hammond himself to escort us to York, via the Gorebeck Asylum of course, to drop me off first, that is?' Martha's words made Abigail feel rather stupid, thoughtless even. But she did not like her maid's sarcasm or her tone. Abigail felt that the woman should have more compassion for her mistress's situation. After all, she had never done anything like this before.

'I didn't think . . . sorry,' Abigail muttered, as Cook returned looking even more flustered than she was before she left them. She gave Abigail a huge hug, almost suffocating her with her ample bosom.

Martha looked at her as she was released from Cook's grip. 'Look Abigail . . . miss, let me do the thinking and you just watch and learn. From this moment on, you're entering my world.

It's not nice and cosy, like yours. It's dirty and you've no experience of it. So stay quiet, keep up and be prepared to learn a few hard facts!'

Abigail stared at her. She had every inclination to tell Martha what to do with 'her world' but what had hurt her the most was that she spoke the truth. Beyond Beckton Manor and the occasional visits to friends of her father's on their estates, she knew nought of the outside, nor should she ever have needed to. It was not expected of her, but now that naivety was equal to ignorance. She controlled her indignation as she was well aware that life in Mr Hackman's world would be a far bleaker option. Abigail was trapped between two harsh choices so she ignored her servant's insubordination and turned her back to her.

She kissed the cook's cheeks and the woman gave in to her tears and ran sobbing to her own room.

Martha sighed heavily. 'We best be going. This isn't easy for any of us. But

Abigail,' Martha put out a hand to her, 'you have to be strong.'

Abigail looked at the offered hand and thought for a second of rejecting it, but changed her mind. She took it in hers, stared at Martha — eye to eye, and said, 'I am.'

3

The coach pulled over at the side of the road. Joshua saw a young girl wrapped in a worn out shawl with scuffed boots and gripping a small bundle. The captain strained to see. 'What is the meaning of this? We're not at an inn yet!'

'Highwaymen!' exclaimed the lady from the other side of her husband.

The man of fashion paled.

Joshua took the initiative. 'I'll find out what the problem is. Please, let's calm ourselves and not overreact.' He opened the door and jumped down, winced, shutting it before the captain could decide to follow.

'Do we have a problem, sir?' he shouted up to the driver.

'Please, I have a coin, I only wish to sit atop.' The young girl's lip was almost quivering. She kept glancing back as if she was terrified she would be seen from the inn. Joshua heard movement from inside the carriage.

The driver looked at him. 'I shouldn't.'

Joshua took hold of her small makeshift sack and tossed it to the man. He then lifted the girl so that she could put her foot on the plate and scramble up.

'If her coin is not enough I will pay her fare to York. At least you shall have some company.'

The driver tipped a finger to his forehead and seated the girl on the open seats.

The door of the carriage opened. Before the captain could step out, Joshua stood ready to climb back in. A small voice drifted down, 'Thanks, mister.'

Joshua smiled then winced again as he put pressure on his leg.

Who or what the girl was, he had no idea, but she was in trouble, of that he was sure. He could smell it a mile off. He had not seated himself before the coach lurched forward and he closed his eyes as he almost fell back onto the bench seat. Now what had he been dreaming about . . . Yes, making a new start, free of the past and all baggage. Who then was the girl and why had he just landed himself possibly with some baggage — even temporarily.

* * *

Abigail followed Martha across the yard. The frosty cobbled ground was slippery and both women ended up stumbling as they approached the stable block. Martha stopped just inside the large stone building's solid oak doors. She put her fingers to her mouth and looked at Abigail, who was just about to speak to her. If there was to be no carriage and no noise why should they come to the stables; it made no sense to Abigail.

She dutifully silenced her thoughts, not voicing one of them, and watched as Martha made her way along the uneven flagged stone floor; each arch in turn housed a separate stall. She turned around to ask Martha what they were doing here, but her maidservant had disappeared.

Abigail moved slowly forward peering into each stall until she reached the last one. She looked inside it, only to be faced with an irate looking Martha, who pressed her finger to her lips once more, after waving it in annoyance at her mistress's slow progress.

She pointed to the drab coloured wagon with its large scarlet coloured wheels and loose canvas cover. The wagon filled up most of the stall, spacious as it was.

'They'll hear that move for sure.' Abigail's voice was no more than a whisper, as she spoke into Martha's left ear. 'Who's going to hitch up the horse to it?'

'Not inside it, behind it,' Martha said, winking at her and grinned.

Abigail followed Martha as she scurried along the side of the stall and felt the wooden panel at the back.

Releasing a catch, the panel moved. Martha used a tinderbox that had been left in the wagon to light an oil lamp. 'Follow me,' she said, still grinning at Abigail's obvious surprise.

Abigail followed, wondering what else existed in her home that she was totally unaware of. She soon found herself in a narrow stone room with some stacked kegs. Martha closed the panel behind them.

'Abigail, we have to climb down some steep stairs.' Martha gestured toward an opening in the earthen wall.

'To where?' Abigail asked, intrigued.

'You'll see soon enough.'

Martha led the way to the corner of the room where stone stairs took them downwards. Abigail did soon see, for the stairs led them down to a natural cavern.

'What is this place?' Abigail asked.

The passage around them broadened out and Abigail could see they were in a sort of cave. Father had warned her about the woods, often telling her tales of ghosts and goblins that could fool a child and imprison them in the underground caverns. 'That's beautiful,' Abigail said as the light rebounded off the wall of the cave.

Martha shrugged. 'That's as maybe, but we've no business down here so the sooner we is out of here, the healthier it will be for us.' She continued to climb up the stairs that had been built into the side of the natural cavity. Abigail could see daylight ahead of them.

'We follow the steps up here, which will bring us out onto the edge of the moor near the road. From there we can walk the mile to the Old Cock Inn. We shall catch the late coach to York.'

Martha blew out the lamp and left it on a ledge for the next person to enter the tunnel to find. Abigail was amazed that these comings and goings had been happening on her own estate without her knowledge. Martha climbed the last few steps to walk out onto a wooded path from between two huge boulders. Both women were breathing deeply as the ascent had been long and steep, but now in the cold open air with the silvery moonlight glistening off the dale, they could look back down on the manor beneath.

Abigail stared at the hidden entrance and tried to commit it to her memory. She had no way of knowing if she would ever return to this place, but something told her she should always remember her way back home.

'There is no going back, Abigail. What is done is done. Childhood has come to an abrupt end right here and now.' The truth in Martha's words was harsh, but she looked upon Abigail kindly.

'I have not been a child, Martha, for quite some time,' Abigail insisted.

'You are not yet one and twenty, so let's just say it's your time to grow up properly now.'

'Martha!'

'We'll walk a mile or so to the inn. They'll give us shelter until the coach is due, then we can talk more freely and in the comfort and warmth.' Martha picked up the bags and set off down the edge of the old road.

Abigail walked alongside her, lifting her bag out of the woman's hand, firmly. Martha seemed to give it up willingly this time.

'Does Father know about the stables?' Abigail asked. She stared up at the moon, then around her at the barren beauty of the moor and, shivering, realised that this was the first time she had ever stepped outside her gilded cage.

'What's wrong, Abigail?' Martha asked her, panting slightly, ignoring the question about Lord Hammond.

'You're quite correct, Martha. My whole life has been that of a pampered child. I know nothing of the reality of life beyond the estate.' Abigail felt a strange sensation — not fear, but what she could only describe as excitement, the thrill of a challenge. She had an important mission; a clear goal to achieve, to get to York and help her father. But more than that, she had to help herself and she could only do that if she unravelled the mystery of her own past . . . for that was what she intended to do. Abigail had to find out who her mother was, or what for that matter; she had the right to know. However, Lord Hammond would always be to her her real father. She had known no other.

'Well, it's better that you realise it now, Abigail. You have to follow my lead. They will not give you the respect and love you have had at the manor. There are more 'Mr Fredericks' in the world than people like yerself, lass. Now, we must make all speed if we are to meet the York coach. Don't be frightened, Abigail. You're not alone — I'm here, and we'll stay together.'

'I know, but in a way I'm really not scared, except for what will happen to Father.' She thought of his last words to her. 'But, Martha, you can tell me who my mother was as we walk along.'

'No, lass, that I can't,' Martha exclaimed.

'Why ever not? You knew her — didn't you?'

'Yes, I did. But I can't walk and talk, not if we're to reach the coaching inn in time,' Martha explained.

'Sorry, I didn't think . . . but you will tell me soon, won't you?'

'Oh yes, but let me catch me breath now, lass. I'm not as young as you.'

Abigail patted her maid's shoulder, knowing that she was older, stronger and wiser than she was. When Martha decided the time was right, she would tell her. Until then, Abigail realised that she would have to be patient, wait and, strange as the idea was to her, it was she who would have to learn to listen and obey.

The uneven ground and bitterly cold night air made their progress slow. The only light to guide them was by the glow of a crescent moon, the stars and a cloudless sky. After half walking and almost running what must have been over a mile, the light suddenly started to leave them as thick menacing clouds moved across the sky, taking their view away with it. Martha had quickened her step. Her breath was heavier and she kept looking nervously up as the world around them darkened.

'What is it, Martha? Do you think it is going to rain?' Abigail asked, as she increased her own pace to keep up with her companion.

'It might, but that's going to be the least of our problems if what I fear is right. It will be worse than a soaking.' Martha was almost running, her ample figure light of foot, but obviously short on breath.

'What is that? We can not get lost if the inn is on this road, for the road is straight and the inn will be large and well lit. Won't it?' People stayed in them so Abigail presumed it would be like a small hall, with an arch for carriages to go through to the stabling block. Martha gave her a stern look that made Abigail think that perhaps her image of the building may not be accurate.

'Tis a bad omen, or I'll be damned.'

'What is a bad omen?' Abigail asked. She was nervous of all the strange animal noises which disturbed the silence of the night, but that was just nature doing what it did — not something Abigail would consider an 'omen'.

'A bad omen is something that'll bring you no good luck and . . . '

'I know what an 'omen' is, Martha.' Abigail shook her head in disbelief that her maid thought her to be so stupid. 'What is it that you have seen and think is one?'

'Them clouds up there — look!' Nervously the woman pointed upwards but soon took her gaze back to the solid ground beneath their feet. The sky was all but dark, the stars and the moon lost above a gloomy shroud. She would not look left or right across the moor, nor stare into the cloak of darkness around them. A strange sound, a bird or some small beast shrilled and Martha let out a gasp of fear before running a few breathless steps.

'Don't worry, Martha, it will pass and then it will be the dawn and another day will begin — a new and a very different one.' Abigail glanced back along the road into an unseen existence, one that was as lost to her now as it was from her sight. She jumped slightly when Martha put a hand out firmly gripping her shoulder.

'Aye, a new dawn, lass, and one that bodes ill as the signs are not good for us. God protect us, for this is to be the darkest dawn I've ever seen.' Martha released her grip and started along the road at her brisk pace.

'Then we need not fear, Martha, for we shall pray for His light to shine and guide our way. Besides, it is always darkest before the dawn, everyone knows that.' Abigail boldly took the lead, carrying her case and struggled on with her head held high. She would survive this; they would make their future work. No one, Frederick or a total stranger, be he suitor or not, would determine her fate; certainly not a mass of cloud or the call of an animal, no matter how menacing it may be.

As the icy rain started to fall she saw something in the distance — a flicker of some sort of light.

'Look, Martha, look! Do you see it? A long building, a barn perhaps and it has a light within it.' Abigail felt a surge of excitement stir inside her. She could not allow her mind to dwell on her father's predicament. She had to be decisive in her thinking. The best she could do for him was to deliver his message to his friend, the solicitor in York, and stay safe until she could return to her beloved home once more. 'Perhaps the farmer who lives here would take us to the inn if I paid him for his trouble, Martha,' Abigail said enthusiastically, thinking about a warm fire, food and a softly upholstered chair.

'That's it, lass.' Martha coughed. 'That 'barns' the inn.'

Abigail sensed a tone of sarcasm in Martha's voice.

'We've made it before the coach.

Hurry now, before . . . ' Martha looked around her anxiously, 'we catch our death of cold, or something carries us off across that moor . . . ' Martha shivered.

Abigail stared at the building again. She was determined not to let her ignorance or naivety show again; she would learn. 'I thought you were the worldly one, Martha? Come on before we catch a chill, there's nothing more than that out here to catch, woman!'

Abigail did not pause to hear her maid's answer. She strode boldly onwards. They approached the inn but, before they knocked on the door, Martha took hold of her mistress's bag.

'This is my world; don't forget it, Miss Abigail. I'll do the talking and you settle and be still,' Martha ordered.

Abigail said nothing. She did not approve of her servant's high handed manner. If she thought that she was going to take over then Abigail decided, rashly, that she would show her she was mature enough to take charge of her own destiny. If not she may as well become the maid, so she waited silently. They heard the heavy latch lift and the door opened.

The figure who greeted Abigail once the old oak door was unbolted caused her to stare in amazement. The tall, skeletal man was attired in breeches, coat, totally dressed in black, as if he was a priest or something dour.

Abigail spoke. 'Good day, I require a warm place to rest for myself and my maidservant until the York coach arrives.'

Martha glared at her, but Abigail ignored her.

'Oh, do you, lass?' The man's voice was deep and powerful, in stark contrast to his wiry frame and appearance. He was obviously humoured by her words. 'Then perhaps you'd best come in out of the cold night air and sit by the hearth.'

Abigail hesitated as the inn was dark and stank of tallow candles. Martha nudged her forwards. She stepped over the muddy threshold and nearly tripped on the raised flagstone edge. Her eyes adjusted to the dimness of the narrow passage. The man closed the door on the right that led to a small parlour and shone the lantern through a narrow shelved passage to the left. Abigail smelt the ale from the dispensary ahead of her. To her left was the hearth; a black range hung with a cauldron and flat iron was flanked by two bench seats against the wall of the inn. There was an upper level that Abigail could see was accessible by a narrow twisting wooden staircase ahead of her, beyond the oak table to her left.

The fire flickered low in the hearth. He took off his hat and, with the exaggerated bow, pointed to the wooden settle built against the outer stone wall. Gratefully, she sat at the end nearest the fire and warmed her hands.

Martha dropped their baggage and crouched by the fire.

Abigail tried not to look frightened as she saw a scar etched into his cheek. 'Would it be possible for us to have something warm to drink, sir, and could you inform me as to how long we need to wait before the stagecoach arrives?' Abigail asked the man.

'Now, about your drink, I do not know, miss. But the coach will be here in less than an hour, and if you're lucky there might even be room for thee inside it. Best I get the landlord and ask him about yer victuals, eh?' The man winked at Martha, who did not look at all amused.

Abigail's mouth dropped open slightly as she had presumed the man was the landlord. She watched him as he casually walked away through the door that led to the dispensary and cellar.

'So are you proud of yourself?' Martha snapped.

'I don't know what you mean, Martha. I think you have forgotten yourself. You are still supposed to be my maid. I requested a warm fire and look, we have one. I know not who the man is but he surely must be attached to the inn, in some way.' Abigail sat bolt upright, her warmed hands resting on her damp coat; she saw steam start to rise from the hem and moved her legs slightly away from the direct heat.

Martha stared defiantly at her. 'No, you have no idea who that man is and 'tis best for your health that it remains so. Now, until we get into polite society again, may I suggest you keep that little mouth of yours firmly shut!'

'Martha! How dare you!' Abigail heard laughter.

A ruddy faced, round figure of a man appeared from the steps.

'Now, tell me, lass, what lady roams around the moors at this hour demanding me fire and victuals?' He stood, hands on hips, and squared up to Abigail who looked pale and lost as she saw another figure blocking the doorway from them.

'Ezekiel Bickerstaff, it is I, Martha Napp, and I don't want to set foot on that coach unless I have a hot drink in me first. Leave the lass alone, she's fresh out of the nursery and don't know any better.' Martha stood up and

Abigail sat mortified as they flung their arms around each other — two rotund, happy figures embracing and kissing like long lost friends — no, Abigail thought, more than that, lovers. Abigail watched silently, appalled. Tears filled Martha's eyes as they recounted how long it had been since last she was at the inn.

'Nearly two seasons gone,' Ezekiel answered her.

Martha shook her head in denial. 'No, it can't be, really. Fetch that drink man, before I get all soft again, and another for Miss Abigail.'

'Aye, lass. So tell me what you're doing here on a night like this. Firstly, though, take this'un upstairs. I'll send her a tray and she can rest safe and sound, out of harm's way, whilst we talk.'

'Aye, all right, Ez.' Martha showed a reluctant Abigail up the narrow twisting stairs into what looked to Abigail like the loft space. Open thatch was above her head. Two truckle beds were built into the eaves of what Abigail felt she had first thought of rightly as a barn. Above each adjoining bed, end to end, was a board to stop the dust and insects falling onto those who slept below on the straw filled mattresses. Immediately to her right was a low arch beneath the cruck frame of the building that led, she presumed, to another bed chamber, as she could hear someone snoring.

'Don't go wakin' up me guests. We will call you when the coach arrives.'

Ezekiel held Martha's hand and led her back down the stairs. Abigail was left with a small oil lamp which flickered as her hand shook. She felt fear like she had never known before. She stared out of the small leaded window at floor level at the inn's gable end and waited patiently for the coach to arrive. Ale, bread and cheese were brought to Abigail and she was left on her own to stare at a dwindling light, and reflect upon the day's events.

She ate without appetite and drank the noxious fluid, realising she knew nothing of the world in reality, only the theory learned from her father's books. She could not help thinking how next time she would stay silent when a strange door was opened, until she could see what or who lay behind it.

A loud dragging noise of barrel over stone could be heard from the lower parlour. Abigail stared down as there were gaps between the planks that made up the floor. She thought of walking down the stairs to see what they were doing, bored with her own company and curious as to who worked at such an hour in such a solitary place. She peered down the stairs but saw that the man in the black tall hat, smoking a long clay pipe, was sitting on the bottom two steps. Abigail stepped back. The sooner she was away from this place the happier she would be. This was not how it should be. It was not how it was going to be. When she arrived at York, Martha Napp was in for a surprise. Abigail was determined she would take control again — but didn't quite know how.

4

Martha returned to Abigail after what seemed like an age. The noises from the lower room had ceased and whoever had been there, other than the grey-faced man, had left by a back door. Abigail was frightened. Every shadow, every snore from the other part of the loft room unnerved her. She was used to high plastered ceilings, polished furniture and fine things, not a draughty open thatch roof with roughly hewn beds beneath it. This, she thought, was a place for insects, spiders and mice. She had been secreted away and guarded like a criminal. Her annoyance with Martha was growing by the minute. Abigail reasoned, she should be better off on her own.

Slowly she retraced her steps back down the narrow wooden stairs, trying not to catch her bonnet on the low ceiling rafter. Abigail stared at the dying fire in the grate as she returned to the parlour, pondering what she would do if that was the case — her new life, vulnerable and exposed to a world she hardly knew nor understood; contemplating being able to make all the decisions for herself. But try as she might she had no answers as to how she could survive like that, as her knowledge of life was so limited. Suddenly, everything that had been seen as a virtue in her life had turned into something which had sufficed to blinker her from truth — reality itself. One thought permeated her gloom, though — I shall learn. She sat down on the bench seat and stared at the dying embers. 'Like a phoenix,' she muttered to herself, 'I shall rise to face the challenge.'

'Lass, what will I do with you? Honestly!' Martha crossed the stone floor and picked up a poker from its stand by the fire. She prodded the ashes and rekindled the subsiding flames.

'Could you not see that that needed doing?'

Abigail was distracted. 'You left me alone!' She did not look at the man who had returned with Martha, but let the woman's rebuke pass over her, and instead stared curiously at the lower parlour door.

Ezekiel stood boldly in front of her. He smelt of sour sweat and ale, his figure was grubby, unshaven and solid as it blocked her view. 'You best be changing your ways and quick, miss. Life has done you a bad turn, but you've got to look out for each other now. You can't be leaving everything to Martha. She is going to need your help too. Life is tough for women with no men folk around. Keep your sights on what is happening about you, and to you — around the both of you that is, and off that what is none of your concern. That way you just might survive to see your majority.' His voice was deep and gruff.

Abigail was going to reply in kind to

the man for talking to her so bluntly. She glared at Martha for leaving her and telling a stranger the details of her current situation. She did not take kindly to being advised as to how to behave or what to do by a common innkeeper.

'Don't look at me like that, Abigail,' Martha answered, more shocked than annoyed.

Abigail noticed that she was already being addressed as an equal or subordinate. It annoyed her, but she was no longer on her father's estate, so she had to adapt her ideals.

'Ezekiel and I go back a long way,' Martha continued and winked at the man, a knowing grin appeared on her face. 'If we can't get on that coach tonight then it is he who will arrange our transport to safety. We mustn't be found, not now. It would be devastating for the both of us. That Hackman man would treat you like . . . well, never you mind. Bad, though, and I'd be thrown into the asylum or the lock up. No, believe me, lass, his sort don't like losing. They is bully boys, no more, no less.'

Abigail glanced at Ezekiel. It was a description which she felt would have fitted the landlord, although she did not voice her opinion. Martha replaced the poker and sat down next to Abigail placing the young woman's hand in her own. Abigail looked straight at the man, dirty and rough as he was and tried to think of him as a friend. She found the idea difficult to come to terms with. Martha had always been hers — her maid, her friend, her servant. Abigail had not known she even had a man friend. She took a deep breath and graciously offered him her hand. 'Then I am both thankful and indebted to you.'

Ezekiel took her kid-gloved hand in his and kissed the back of it, bowing low as he did. 'It is I who am honoured, miss.'

Martha laughed and Abigail managed a smile in what had been so far the most traumatic night of her life, although she had to admit there was something about the man that was good-naturedly humorous — when he tried to be.

'Ez', it's coming.' A little old lady with only one tooth visibly left in her head peered around the corner of the doorway. A floppy cloth bonnet framed her craggy face.

'Thanks, Maude.' Ezekiel sighed deeply and looked at them both. 'Whatever is to become of you, Martha? I wish you a good and safe journey. You've been a precious sight for my poor failing eyes.'

'Get away, man, you always was a flatterer and I bet you've sight like a hawk.' She patted his arm, but there was a longing in her eyes that was plain for Abigail to see; Martha loved this man.

'It's been too long.' He kissed her full on the mouth and Abigail looked away, not able to cope with this new side of Martha. Her relationship with Martha was special to her. Abigail had never known a life without her being there and she realised she was jealous of this man, because of the open fondness that Martha showed him in her every gesture. Jealousy was an emotion she felt quite ashamed of. There was so much about Martha, like her own past, that Abigail did not know. Everything that had been solid as a rock in her life seemed to have become lucid.

'Aye, that's as maybe,' Martha answered him, 'I'll be back one day, honest.' Martha gave him one last hug.

He stared at Abigail with no hint of humour. 'Have you any idea what this woman gave up for you?'

Abigail guessed the answer would be 'him'.

'Now, now, Ez! I'll have none of that. Best be on our way,' she said, looking around fondly at Abigail.

Abigail tried to return an affectionate smile before she walked into the passage and waited by the threshold as the great stagecoach thundered to a halt outside the inn. Abigail was aware of a strange fluttering feeling in the pit of her stomach. Her new life started here.

'May God be with us.' Martha was staring at the darkening sky, concern on her face.

'It's all right, Martha, only a storm, no more nor less,' Abigail whispered.

'You don't understand. There are things out there, on the moors. Strange goings on. Tis not fit for a Christian to be out on a night like this.' Martha looked pale.

'Then have more faith in God than the things 'going on' and we will be fine.' She heard the sharp intake of breath Martha took, but could not reply as Abigail had stepped outside the inn into the night.

Abigail considered that there was enough for them to worry about with what they could see in this world, without looking for ghosts and demons or whatever it was that filled Martha's imagination. Abigail had no time for such notions. They were fantastic tales made only to scare children with, and she was no longer a child.

She saw Ezekiel hand a flagon of ale to the driver. He held out an oil lamp in their direction. At first Abigail thought it was to light their way, but then she realised it was to show the driver his new passengers. Reluctantly, the man nodded and drank a swig of the ale before climbing down.

He opened the door of the coach and leaned in slightly. 'We has two ladies needing seats. Could one of you gents go up top and let them inside?' The driver turned to Ezekiel. 'They can pay to be inside can't they?'

'Of course — I'd hardly ask you now, would I, if they couldn't?' Ezekiel smiled affably.

A soldier of the militia looked out of the carriage window. 'Let the maid go atop. That is no place for a gentleman to be seated!' The man sitting next to him nodded.

Ezekiel stepped forward, but Abigail spoke out. She knew the man's mentality all too well — servants should be visible when needed, yet invisible when not. 'I'll sit above. Martha, you ride inside.'

'No, miss, you'll catch your death.' Martha held onto her arm, as she looked anxiously up to the full height of the stage. Abigail did not cherish the thought either, but it was a chance to shame the gentlemen, and hopefully spur them into a more noble action.

A tall figure alighted from the other side of the carriage. Abigail saw as he came around the back of the coach that he was wearing a caped greatcoat and hat, the gentleman strode around to where Abigail and Martha were standing. He had a slight uneven step to his gait.

'I will ride above.' He spoke with an air of authority, a confident and educated voice.

Abigail looked straight at the man. However, between his hat and the high collar of his coat there were little of his features she could see clearly in the dimness of the night. She thought he might have very dark hair, or it could have been a trick of the lamp's light. He climbed above to take his position on the upper seat.

Thank you . . . sir,' Abigail shouted up to him, 'You are truly a kind and thoughtful gentleman!'

She thought she heard him chuckle. He raised an acknowledging hand to his hat then asked, 'Now can we please continue on our journey?'

Abigail glanced up before entering the carriage. She sensed that he was smiling back at her despite the few drops of rain that had just started to fall.

The driver walked over to the other side of the road.

'Where's he going, Martha?' Abigail whispered to her before using her sense of reasoning.

Martha shook her head, glancing at Ezekiel, who was opening the coach door. Two passengers climbed down from the top of the coach and followed the driver. Abigail blushed as she realised they were relieving themselves. She hoped that, in the dark of night and rain, no one had heard her question or noticed her discomposure.

Abigail felt the hard seat under her, choosing to look out of the window, staring into the emptiness, and swallowed silently. For a moment she thought she saw something move in the gloom. Martha's fears must be rubbing off on her. She must not cry, must not panic, she had to be strong for the both of them. Martha squeezed inside the carriage, half falling onto the narrow seat. Opposite her, a man wearing the poppy coloured jacket of the militia stared pompously back, his plumed hat nestled on his lap. Martha looked down at her own lap and straightened her slightly damp skirt. Abigail was faced by a traveller wearing a fashionable coat. He smiled, moving his legs slightly to accommodate hers, but in the process his knees rubbed against hers in what seemed an intrusive gesture. He smiled,

Abigail tucked her feet as neatly as she could under her seat to avoid any further contact. She rested her head against the side of the stagecoach, smelling the wood and leather polish, hoping it would not affect her on the long journey. The only other passengers, a married couple, stared accusingly at them but uttered no word of protest.

The driver shouted and they moved off at great speed along the rutted road. The stale smell of old smoke from the gentlemen's clothes made Abigail feel uncomfortable. She was used to a great deal of space and open air.

'He drives recklessly,' the militia man spoke out.

'He is anxious to make up time,' the man of fashion answered. 'We have been unexpectedly delayed,' he paused and looked pointedly at Abigail and Martha, 'and the storm that was promised will soon be upon us I fear.'

Indeed, within minutes the storm arrived. Thunder, lightning and heavy rain ensued. Noises echoed in and around the stagecoach, making conversation difficult which, to Abigail, was a blessing, because she had no wish to explain her position to the militia man who eyed her suspiciously. She felt sorry for the man who had nobly given up the relative comfort of the carriage to sit atop a moving coach in the midst of a storm. The sooner they arrived at York the better, and then she could disappear into the background of the city.

* * *

The girl was ill-dressed for such a journey. The coach bumped and jarred as its driver made the best time he could in the worsening conditions. Joshua seated himself next to her and wrapped his coat around both of them. Without objection she nestled into his warmth.

'Who are you running from?'

'You got it wrong. I'm going to see me aunt. She lives in the big city. I . . .'

Joshua pulled away. 'Lie to me girl and you are on your own.'

'Please! Don't let them put me in the debtor's gaol. I only asked the driver to take me as far as my coin would go and I'd have walked the rest. Just so long as he don't find me again.' She held onto his coat tightly.

'You finger my wallet and I'll toss you off here without bothering the driver to stop.'

'You're not slow are you mister, despite being soft like.' She looked up at him with eyes that seemed too wide for her small face. She needed a good feed.

'No, I'm no fool, nor soft. So who are you running from and why?'

'His name is Solomon Petty. He took me in as a child from the orphanage at Whitby. He made me work for him and his wife in their inn but as I started to grow he had other ideas. They both did. They wanted me to do more than wait tables to earn them money. So I've run away. But he'll follow me. He'll come maybe as far as York cos he has contacts and business there.'

'It's a common enough fate . . . what

is your name, girl?'

'Molly. I don't know what as me dad wasn't named.'

'Well, Molly 'Idon'tknowwhat', you will travel to York and we will try and find a safe haven for you.'

'You is a gentleman, sir.'

He laughed and silently cursed the cold and damp as his leg ached the more for it.

* * *

The stagecoach travelled as fast as the driver could safely take it. A part of Abigail could not help but find the whole journey as exciting as it was frightening. She had never experienced such things before. The storm worried Martha who gripped the seat and appeared to Abigail to be deep in prayer. Martha had often told Abigail tales of ghosts and demons — hobgoblins that inhabited the cliffs along the infamous jagged northeast coast, but she had never thought for one moment Martha actually believed in any of them.

Dawn slowly broke but, with the thick cloud and heavy rain it was indeed a dismal affair. The moors were drab, or invisible, lost in the mist as the stagecoach journeyed on and passed fields and villages. Then the sky cleared for a short while just enough for her to see the great towers of a gothic cathedral in the distance across the vale.

She nudged Martha and smiled at her, trying to snap her back into the more relaxed composure that she was used to seeing. Martha seemed unwilling to lift her mood.

As they approached the city walls, houses with tall brick facades and sash windows with fashionable fanlights lined their way. They passed a convent and Abigail wondered if she should hide from the world in there, but decided it was not for her. Later the screams from the dreaded asylum drifted by as the doors were momentarily opened to let in a new admission. It was more daunting to Abigail than anything she had ever seen before in her life. The thought of Martha being sent to such a place to work, horrified her and she cringed at the gravity of their predicament. There, lunatics were housed pitifully; once in, there was little chance of being released. Martha recoiled on the seat and Abigail held her hand firmly. They would never put her Martha in there as a worker or inmate — never! Frederick was a powerful man and, sadly, a dangerous enemy.

Beyond the stone and crumbling city walls lay their future. Through the old medieval gates she could see the timbered buildings of an older style which, to Abigail, as the coach slowed to a halt, were as murky as the narrow roads, fouled as they were by horse, cattle, sheep and man alike. The stagecoach stopped outside an inn and the door opened. They alighted into a strange world. 'Oh Lord,' she said her silent words within her own mind, 'make our way simple, safe and clear.'

Rain poured down and Abigail was grateful for the step and the wooden board that the innkeeper of the tavern placed on the mud splattered ground as she climbed down. Above them, the phoenix painted on the inn board swung in the strong wind, unnoticed as the anxious travellers made for the shelter of the tavern; however, to Abigail it gave comfort for it seemed to be a sign that all would be well. Stepping inside the tall narrow building was a strange experience for her.

The morning was young, and light struggled to break through the bleak sky outside. Inside the Phoenix Inn, Abigail looked around her, breathing in the stale air. Flames flickered in their lamps and a young serving girl bobbed a curtsey in front of her.

'Would you like some food, ma'am . . . miss?' she asked, and pointed to a table behind her.

Cold pie, cheese and bread had been arranged on pewter platters ready for the tired travellers to purchase. Martha stepped forward before Abigail could answer and enquired after a room in which her mistress may refresh herself.

Abigail's attention had returned to her fellow passengers alighting from the stagecoach. She looked for the gentleman in the caped coat who had so kindly climbed atop the carriage in order that she and Martha could travel inside together. Abigail saw him climb down a step, resting his foot on the wheel then jump the rest of the way to the ground. He was strong, yet as he landed his balance went slightly as his leg gave way under him. He propped himself against the coach to prevent himself falling. She was filled with guilt at the state of his appearance. He must be ill or injured in some way — perhaps lame even.

She ignored the plump man of fashion and the pompous officer of the militia as they passed her by — her existence equally ignored by them. Their eyes were firmly fixed on the food and ale.

When the wet gentleman entered the tavern, his greatcoat dripping with the icy rain, Abigail was filled with feelings of gratitude to him.

'Sir . . . would you allow me to purchase a repast for you as a thank you for your kindness.' Abigail smiled at his surprised expression.

He removed his hat carefully so as not to drip water onto her pelisse. A raggedy figure who had alighted also entered the inn behind him. In the dimness of the tavern's light his deep brown eyes looked back at her with what Abigail thought were curiosity and a glint of humour. She could not help but admire his handsome face surrounded by unruly dark hair.

'It was a pleasure to get some . . . ' he glanced at the window with its small leaded panes, which were being lashed by streaks of heavy rain, ' . . . fresh air. The coach's interior was becoming quite stuffy.' He stared somewhat pointedly towards their travelling companions.

'Then at least let me repay the difference of your journey's fare. It is not right you should be inconvenienced as well as out of pocket,' Abigail persisted.

'Please think nothing of it. It was the very least I could do.' He grinned pleasantly at her.

Abigail did not know how to reply to him as she had not expected him to refuse her offers. She felt small standing next to him, and quite lost as she realised her words had perhaps been forward and inappropriate.

The young girl stood at the side of him. 'Begging your pardon, sir . . . but I wanted to say thank you for your kindness also.'

'There is no need, come let us eat something warm.' He looked at Abigail. 'You must excuse us unless you would care to join us for a meal?'

'My maid is making arrangements, sir.'

The girl at his side took her small pink hand and slipped it into his.

'Come, Molly, we shall eat and then find your home.'

'Miss Hammond,' Martha bustled up to her giving the stranger a wary look, 'A room is ready for you now.'

He bowed slightly to her before walking over to the innkeeper. Abigail saw him down a tankard of ale and purchase some food and take the young girl over to a quiet corner of the inn.

Martha gave Abigail's arm a nudge. 'Talking to strange men in taverns, lass! Whatever next?'

'You talked with one not so long ago as I recall, Martha,' Abigail snapped back at her. She faced Martha. 'In fact you threw yourself into his arms as I recall.'

'That was quite different. We is old friends,' Martha answered in a vexed manner.

Abigail felt tired, and her Martha looked it too. Both, Abigail realised, were somewhat daunted by the turn of events in their lives and, if she was honest with herself, she was very scared. The latter was a feeling she was fighting against. Abigail's change of circumstance, environment and lowered position in life, felt like a burden that was extremely heavy to bear. She had never been one to give way to a pique of temper, however. Martha carried their bags into the small dark room and Abigail shut the door firmly behind her.

She stared in disgust at the old, threadbare hangings around the four poster bed.

'Martha Napp, now we have some privacy, at last. As we rest you must tell me who I am. I can not wait a moment longer. I need to know the truth!'

5

Joshua removed his sodden coat. Molly clung to her small bag; her skirt and hair were wet. She looked cold and scared. He put a drink and a plate of stew in front of her. 'Eat, Molly, then we will talk.'

Large blue eyes, with heavy tired lids looked at him. She nodded and ate, all the time looking at the door as if a monster might appear. Once finished, he sat back on the settle and studied her. 'Do you know anyone in York?'

She shook her head.

'Do you have any more money?'

She shook her head.

He looked at her worn clothes, her battered ill-fitting boots and leaned forwards.

'What did you expect to do in York, Molly?'

'I thought I'd get a job in a big

house. Maybe work in a kitchen where there was a warm fire and plenty of food. Then I'd work so hard that after a while I'd be made up to a housemaid and then an upstairs maid and one day I'd . . . ' Her face had become animated, a sparkle lit her tired and eyes. Molly stopped speaking, replaced the spoon on an empty plate and hugged her small bundle to her, then looked down.

'Then what?' Joshua asked, curious where her ambitions would end.

'I dream too much. I always have. I get beaten for daydreaming, yet I still do it.' She shrugged her shoulder, 'I'm sorry.'

'Don't apologise for wanting to improve your lot through hard work. What comes after you become a housemaid?'

'I fall in love with the butler and he marries me.' She blushed.

'Your dream, Molly, would have become a nightmare by nightfall today if you had not stumbled into my path. Stay here, I will book a room and we shall sort this out tomorrow when I am rested.' He went to stand up. His leg was stiff. When Joshua placed his hand on the table to ease his weight up, she touched his hand. 'Mr I . . . I don't want to . . . I'll find somewhere don't bother, please.' Her voice was shaky.

'Molly you are little more than a child. I am booking a room and if we are lucky you shall have a servant's cot brought in, for your own safety, not for any other reason. If you leave here now, or worse, stay in an inn on your own, you will end up as a whore before morning and may graduate to a thief within the week. I will not hurt or abuse you.'

'How can I repay you?'

'You can go straight to sleep and give me some peace because I have a long journey to London tomorrow.'

She sat hugging her bundle as he sorted out the room and had his bag carried upstairs. There were no servant's cots but there was a big armchair by an open fire. He asked for extra blankets and two bowls of warm water, towel and soap.

'Molly, sort yourself out. I will be downstairs long enough for you to freshen up, dry your hair and make yourself comfy in the chair.' She nodded. 'Don't touch my things, Molly. I'll show you trust, cross me once and I will have you arrested.'

'I won't, sir. You is kind and I need a friend.'

* * *

Martha dropped their bags down on the bare wood floor and walked over to the small fire which had been lit to air the room. It failed miserably. The room smelt stale and fusty. Old drapes were nailed to a beam, as opposed to hung at the ill-fitting window, and swung back unevenly, to be held in place by worn out ties.

'There's no good getting all angry at me, Miss Abigail.' Martha was most indignant.

'Why ever not? There seem few others who I can be annoyed with. You

86

have lied to me for as long as I have known you. My whole life is not what I thought it was. I have no idea who I am or where I came from. Everything I thought was true, all I believed was so, has no truth in it at all. Was my mother a lady or a . . . wanton woman? I have a right to know and I must be told the truth for I shall never have peace in my heart again if I do not.' Abigail could not remember ever speaking to Martha in such a way.

'What's been done in your life was done for your own good — and what's more, my girl, what's done is done and can't be changed. If it has been so important, why has it taken you to your twentieth year before raising a question about it?' Martha's colour was high; her ruddy cheeks betrayed how upset she was by Abigail's change of manner.

Abigail, however, was determined to find out the truth. How could she be her own person and survive in the world if her real identity was being kept from her. Nothing made sense to her anymore; it was as if she had lived a lie, a life that was, apparently, not rightly hers. Frederick's words echoed in her mind; he had referred to her bad blood. Was it true? How was she to know? But Martha did, and Abigail stared sternly at her.

'Because I believed I was from an almshouse where there were no records of who my parents were. Because I believed you would tell me if there was more to tell and because I was so happy with my life that I didn't even care!'

'That being the most important point, miss. You were happy with your lot and few can boast that fact.' Martha sighed and crossed her arms firmly in front of her. 'Abigail, most folk around those parts — where you were found, would have left you to meet your maker in the abbey grounds, whether they had been rich or poor. The poor could not have fed another mouth and the rich would not even have blinked at you as they sped by in their fancy coaches. Your life would have been forfeited.

Folks believe it would have been your fate and they would've looked the other way. It took a special kind of person to do what Lord Hammond did. He's different to most of his type, God bless him. He took you despite you being a bastard. Admittedly he'd intended to feed you up and then let you go to the foundling home, but by the time you thrived he was already besotted by your charms and to the young life that had nearly been snuffed out all too early . . . Like his wife, Georgiana and his own bairn.'

'Tell me what happened to her, Martha . . . please?' Abigail tried to soften her voice slightly, hoping it would encourage Martha to reveal the secrets of her past.

'She died with her babe, a girl, only one year before you were found; neither had stood a chance. The baby was all the wrong ways round within its mother. Tragic . . . really tragic. Anyhow, he found you and did all he could to help you survive, and when you did he made sure you got to live a good life, denied nothing, from learning to riding to being loved.'

'Who am I, though?' Abigail persisted, as she tried to come to terms with what she had just heard.

Martha thought she had explained what would make Abigail feel better. However, to Abigail it raised even more questions and doubts. Did it mean that if her father's real daughter had lived she may have been left to perish? It was a disturbing thought that made her shiver involuntarily. She felt as though she was somehow not quite 'real', but a substitute daughter, no better than a replacement for the child of his own whom he had been denied. All the times she had looked on Frederick as a brother, thinking he considered her as his sister and the true daughter of Lord Hammond, had suddenly lost their credibility. Had she been in the wrong? Was she in fact no more than an impostor — Lord Hammond's pampered pet?

Why had her . . . for the first time she hesitated before even thinking the title . . . her father, not legally acknowledged her? Why had he hesitated?

'Miss Abigail Hammond,' Martha said, and looked to the fire instead of at her. 'That's who you are and that's who you will always be until the day you marry a fine man of your own.'

'Did he ever have papers drawn up to say that, Martha? Did he? Do I exist in law?' Abigail asked, but knew the answer before Martha replied.

'That's what is in the letter — instructions for Mr Ashton at the solicitors' office. He has to get things sorted out and quick like, because Lord Hammond has to be well enough to put things he intended to do years ago in order. He wanted to find a good match for you, but let things slip by as time itself did. Abigail, bless him, he was loathe to let you go. Of all the things in his life that were bad, he always kept you away from it, clean like.'

'Perhaps it was not the real reason.

Perhaps Frederick made my dubious heritage common knowledge — who would want a bastard for a wife? They'd be no better than a laughing stock and I'd be an outcast from polite society. That is the truth of it; he kept me at Beckton to protect me from the harsh reality, my own truth.' Abigail spoke the words filled with bitterness.

'Abigail! How could you even think such things let alone say them! Your father, — yes, that is who he is — Lord Hammond has always been a father to you in the eyes of the world and to you. It's just as well he can not hear you or for sure he would take a turn for the worse, lass.' Martha was waving an accusing finger at her.

Abigail spun around and stared at the flickering fire.

'Then let us go and deliver this letter to Mr Ashton straight away. Then, if we return with him to the manor, all will be put right and we can send Frederick on his way with a firm word in his ear!' Abigail stood up, straightening her hooded cloak and arranging her bonnet.

'I don't like this happening to us any more than you do. It isn't that simple, lass. Mr Frederick Hammond is a man of great influence; he has the law on his side. He knows it well enough. He represents not only your father as his son and heir but the law here too. If that piece of paper your father has given you falls into his hands, he may prove it false or something. Lord Hammond told me we was to deliver it, then take ourselves off somewhere for a few months to see what was to happen next. Abigail, if Mr Hammond can manipulate the situation to his advantage you will have nothing, not even a life of your own to live. I could be locked in that asylum or the assizes. We've got to make the most of what we have with us here.' She warmed her hands over the flames.

'That may be true and I wouldn't put it past Mr Hammond to do such a thing, but we have to try.' Abigail placed her hand on Martha's arm. 'I need to

know who I am, Martha! It is my right!'
Abigail did not raise her voice for she
did not want the whole tavern to know
her business. She wanted this woman to
tell her everything she knew about her
past, no matter what it was. Abigail
then remembered Martha's words.
'What abbey grounds?'

'Sit down, child.' Martha pulled the
one chair in the room over to the fire
and then fetched Abigail's luggage over.
She sat herself on her haunches and
rummaged inside the bag.

'I'm not a child, Martha!'

'Then don't act like one!' Martha
said sharply, and then almost immediately tried to withdraw her outburst.
'I'm sorry, but remember for the next
three months you are still officially one.
So we shall not be staying here very
long as we must lose ourselves — somewhere.' Martha pulled out the Bible
and handed it to Abigail. 'Whitby
Abbey, but it is of no importance.'

Abigail took the Bible and sat down
on the chair. There was a knock on the

door that made her jump nervously.

Martha put a comforting hand on Abigail's shoulder and smiled. 'Come in.' She looked down at Abigail's worried face and explained, 'I ordered us some victuals.'

A tray was left on the small table. Martha went over to it and turned her nose up at the roughly prepared food. 'Cook would have had one of her turns if she knew you was being fed food like this.' She picked up the plate and took it over to Abigail. 'Can't be fussy, lass. Best be eating something, you need to get used to eating what we can when we can. Once Mr Hammond has realised we're missing the first place he'll look is around the estate, then at the stage-coach routes. If he figures out the coaches thereabouts he'll look to Newcastle or York. He knows folks here, so this would be the easiest place for him to ask questions, or should I say, to have questions asked. We had best eat, do your business, then rent a chaise to go elsewhere.' Martha took a large bite of the pie and chewed away merrily on it.

'Why not go to London? We'd never be traced there, would we?' Abigail asked as she opened the Bible and removed the two letters that were hidden inside.

'London, whatever would we do there? That's miles away, that is, with its dens of . . . well, places no decent folk would go.

'Where is the other one?' Abigail lifted out two letters. 'There were three before.'

'That one has already been delivered.' Martha took another big mouthful of the pie. 'Bit stale but not too bad. Here, try some.'

'To whom?' Abigail asked, not going to be side tracked.

'To the inn, of course . . . about our escape.'

Martha was busy munching nervously away at the pie. 'But how did he know I would need to leave like that?' Abigail asked.

'Oh, I expect he covered the option, just in case, like.' Martha continued quickly, 'One of them is for Mr Ashton and the other 'un is for you.' She gulped down some ale. 'Now might be a good time for you to read it, then if you have any questions you want to ask me, I'll answer what I can.'

Abigail put the one addressed to Mr Ashton into her reticule and then opened the one addressed to her.

My Dearest Abigail,

The fact you are reading this means I am either incapacitated or dead. In either case, I beg you to be strong and be happy for your own sake as well as for mine.

You have brought me many years of joy at a time when I grieved for my dear Georgiana, who left me earlier than I could have ever imagined. I found you one terrible night, All Souls Eve, not a night to be caught out in a storm, by old Whitby Abbey. However, it was a place I return to from time to time as Georgiana and I used to visit. God has His plans for us and our paths were destined to cross. You looked pathetic and half starved but even then you had a natural beauty about you and a will to survive. You still have that will and I beseech you to use every ounce of it to carry you through this difficult time.

I hope by the time you read this you will have a husband of your own by your side and little ones running around you, as you did with me. Enjoy each moment of your life as you live it.

I understand your mother was a good lady who succumbed to the charms of a manipulative man. Do not blame her as love is a powerful emotion; it can build or destroy. Love is undoubtedly the greatest gift anyone can have and you have a heart that has given me something I thought was lost to me forever — unreserved love.

*Abigail think not of what we have
lost in our separation but of what we
shared in life. Shed no tears. I pray
we meet once more in heaven.*
Your loving father,
Lord Edmund Horatio Hammond.

Abigail swallowed, choking back the tears that were threatening to overwhelm her tired eyes.

'This still does not tell me who I am. My mother was a good, yet fallen, woman. Who was my real father, other than a manipulator and deserter of innocence? So who am I, Martha? You know, I can sense it, you still do not tell me the truth.' Abigail was standing over her maid. Martha did not straighten up. She would not even look up at her.

'Abigail, I was visiting friends in the town. It was late and no one wants to be out when it's nightfall on that night, believe me. It was quiet, except for the noise of the waves as they broke against the harbour, cliff and shore. Whitby has a perpetual motion to it. Silence never really exists, but a scream rang out, then I heard a baby cry. At first I thought it was the screech of a sea bird, but then I heard it again clear as day — or night. He, Lord Hammond, found you dropped by the crumbling walls. Not been there long or the bitter cold of the night would have finished you for sure. The footman was ordered to knock on doors, but no one knew who you were. You needed nursing and I came with you. It was to be a short visit whilst Lord Hammond decided what was to be done with you. Yet, here I am.' She patted Abigail's shoulder. 'Now eat something.'

'So you have no knowledge as to my parentage?' Abigail stared at Martha, who was busying herself with the bags.

'Now isn't that what I've just been saying to you?' Martha moved things around within them as if preoccupied with what she was doing.

Abigail thought of calling her a liar there and then, but decided the time was not right. Martha was not telling her the truth, or not all of it anyway. She wondered why, because it was not like her to lie — to stubbornly refuse, yes, but not to lie.

Abigail put her letter safely away. She would decide what to do next. 'Wouldn't this prove he is my father?'

'No, it was written long since and there is no witness or seal. It could have been copied. I doubt it would stand on its own.'

'I need a black pelisse, a mourning coat and hat. I've decided that whilst I attend Mr Ashton you will find me suitable attire for when we leave this city. I shall be an army widow seeking a new start in life with her maidservant.'

'Will you indeed?' Martha forgot her charade of rummaging and closed the bag. 'And when did you decide this?'

'Just now, while you were telling me your 'story'.' Abigail tilted her head and stared at Martha, but the maid opened her mouth as if to speak then changed her mind and nodded as if it was a reasonable idea.

'And what would you be called?' Martha asked. 'And can I be me or do I have to become a 'Betsy' or someone else.'

Abigail thought of the long cold walk to the Old Cock Inn and the country that surrounded them. 'Mrs Moor.' Abigail grinned, then carefully and thoughtfully folded up her father's letter and placed it back within the pages of his Bible. 'I shall be Mrs Abigail Moor and you may as well be who you are. No one pays attention to maids anyhow and, besides, at least you have the comfort of knowing who you 'really' are.'

'Well it's as good as idea as any,' Martha answered, without rising to Abigail's jibe. 'Best remember, though, liars need to have good memories.'

'Yes, I couldn't agree more. And when we journey to Whitby we will test yours, as you can tell me your 'story' all over again.' Abigail brushed out her hair and was surprised that Martha did not retort. A fact that, to Abigail, proved she was correct.

'Why Whitby?' Martha asked. 'Wouldn't it be better to travel away from any place that is connected with your past?'

'I wish to see the sea,' Abigail answered.

'Abigail, you must trust me now more than you ever have. I've never let you down, ever.' Martha looked quite solemn.

Abigail smiled at her. 'Nor shall you now, but you have to trust me too. I meant it when I said I am no child, I do not wish to be treated like one. Not anymore. There are things we must discuss but, here we have no time and Father needs us to act quickly on his behalf. So let us see to our business and be on our way. Then we shall speak of this again when it is the correct time.' Abigail kissed Martha's cheek. 'Whatever the truth of it, Martha, you have been there throughout my life and for that I give you my love and thanks.'

'Aye, lass, I know, but some things are best left unsaid. No good stirring up what cannot be undone. Settle your sights on your future.' Martha smiled at her.

'Yes, as soon as you've told me what it is that I should leave undone. Then I will settle. Until then I shall never find peace.'

6

Joshua stayed downstairs in the smoky inn. It was busy; all manner of people filled it. He bought himself a drink of porter and sat with his back to the wall. He liked to observe people. His time in the war had taught him to be aware of his surroundings, to be watchful and to always know where the doors were in case he needed to flee to fight another day. The girl's presence was unexpected. He'd seen too many like her. War not only killed men in battle, it destroyed families, young lives ruined before they had the chance to live. This girl, for some reason, touched him. He could not save Francesca but perhaps he could give this waif a life worth living. He rubbed his tired face. He was aware just how sentimental he was becoming. His men would think he'd gone soft, losing the will to fight.

Perhaps he had. Who'd want a lame soldier anyhow?

There was a blast of cold air as a large framed man slipped in, carrying a blackthorn walking stick. He held it six inches below the smooth ball handle, so it was obviously not needed for its normal use. The man stood inside the door and looked around. Rain had soaked his oilskin coat and now trickled down onto the rushes strewn on the wooden floor.

He strode over to the counter. 'I'm looking for a girl!' he announced loudly.

A young woman stepped forward, her breasts spilling out of her dress. She smiled at him and placed both her hands on her hips, baring more of her flesh.

He got hold of her wrist and pulled her ungraciously over to his side. 'Aye, you'll do for later. But it isn't a whore I am looking for. I'm looking for a young lass what's run away from home; answers to 'Molly'.'

The woman tried to pull her arm

away, but he held her fast. 'You offered, now you stay!' A look of fear crossed the tired lackless face of the wench.

The innkeeper stood before him. 'We don't have any young girls here and we doesn't want any trouble, mister.'

'Where's the coach driver? I heard she took a coach.' The man stared around the gloomy room.

The innkeeper glanced at Joshua before answering. 'He, like the coach, has gone on its way. There is no girl staying here.'

'You there, you come in on the coach?' He stared at Joshua. People fell silent.

'Who is it that wishes to know?' Joshua placed his tankard back on the table and stared at the approaching man.

'My name is Amos Drab and I am her guardian.' He walked over to Joshua releasing the woman's arm. She rubbed her bruised skin, where his grip had tightened, and slipped out the back of the inn.

'Yes, I did.'

'You see a young lass? Scrap of a thing clutching a small bag.' Drab was now at his table, towering over Joshua.

'There were two single gentlemen, a married couple, a lady and her maid and my ward and myself. I don't recall a girl.' Joshua stared directly at him, but noticed the lady's maid had come back down the stairs with an empty jug. She had heard him, as had most of the people in the room. He knew she had disapproved of him taking the girl to his room, but her eyes now seemed to be viewing him in a different light.

'Damn that brat! Takes me food and runs. I'll have her publicly flogged when I catch her!' He turned to the innkeeper. 'I need a room and the wench. Send her to me.'

'The rooms are full, sir. You best try down the road,' the innkeeper replied and returned to his counter.

Drab balled a fist and gripped his stick, but three men stood between him and the innkeeper. 'The inn's full,' repeated one of them.

'I'll be back before the London coach goes, and I'll be watching this place.' Drab waved his stick, cursed and left.

Joshua stood up, limping as he made his way to the stairs.

'You did a kindly thing there, sir,' Martha commented as he passed. The younger man smiled at her and winked as he carefully climbed the stairs.

7

Both Abigail and Martha looked nervously around them as neither wanted to be on the open street any longer than they needed to be. They waited by the black door hoping Mr Ashton would be willing to meet them without an appointment. With each passing hour Abigail felt the urgency to leave the city as soon as possible grow. 'Martha, I am grateful for how you handled things at both inns but, here, let me do the talking this time.' Abigail looked at her maid and saw a fleeting smile play on the woman's lips.

'I thought I was to go and leave you on your own whilst I found your mourning attire.' Martha raised an eyebrow at her mistress.

'I think it would look better if I have a servant with me,' Abigail explained. The truth was she was extremely nervous and did not want to be on her own. Martha would be watching her back. Besides, she could hardly be travelling on her own. Martha, she decided, was a poor enough chaperone.

'Funny enough, lass, I'd figured that much out for meself. Now, whilst you're in here do you want me to stay close like, just in case he decides to contact young Mr Hammond?'

'All right, Martha, I didn't heed your words last time and I'm sorry for that, but there is no reason to adopt that attitude with me, is there? Please remember your position and do not call me 'lass' again.' Abigail's rebuke was in a lowered voice, but it lost none of its impact. 'Stay with me. Hopefully, this will not take long then we can leave the city before noon.'

'Good, lass . . . Miss Hammond, I mean. You're learning quick, always have done. As soon as . . . '

The large door was opened by a gentleman dressed from head to toe in black. The cravat around his collar appeared to force his head abruptly upwards. He stared at Martha, before looking at Abigail. 'Can I help you, Miss . . . ?'

'I should like to speak to Mr Ashton, please.' Abigail adopted as formal an air as she could.

'Do you have an appointment, Miss . . . ?' he asked.

Abigail held her head high, looked congenially at the man and answered, 'I am afraid not but I have a letter to deliver to him — by hand.'

'Please enter.' He opened the door wide. 'Who is this person?' He glanced at Martha as he addressed Abigail. The woman flushed and shot him a less than gracious look in return.

'This,' Abigail put a gloved hand on Martha's shoulder, 'is my companion and personal maid. Miss Napp will stay with me, as is her place in life.' Abigail was firm, but pleasant. He escorted them into a mahogany panelled waiting room. Abigail squeezed Martha's shoulder and shot her a warning look. Here was the world of her father — a gentleman's world.

'If you wait here, I shall see if Mr Ashton is able to see you today. Who should I say is delivering the letter and from whom is it sent?' He looked from one to the other as if sizing them up.

'I am the daughter of Lord Edmund Hammond and the letter is from him, directly.' Abigail held the letter firmly within her beaver muffler.

He bowed to her in an overly dramatic fashion and left.

Abigail's face flushed deeply. She felt most uncomfortable and hated the feeling. Other than by her own father, she was beginning to wonder if she was viewed in the outside world merely as a 'bastard' child. Was that how Frederick had let polite society know of her? As the 'runt' her father had taken in, like one would a dog. Martha placed a comforting hand upon hers as if she had read Abigail's thoughts.

'The sooner I become Mrs Moor the better, Martha.'

'Aye, la . . . Miss Abigail. The world's no place for a woman on her own,' Martha agreed.

'Well, it's not fair. Why should I not be able to live my life as I choose as Frederick has chosen his? I am more intelligent than he is.'

'That's as maybe, but the world just ain't made that way. The laws are made by men and for men and they'll never change 'em.'

'Then it's time we made them, Martha.' Abigail resented everything she had accepted as normal up until such a short time ago.

'Now, you concentrate on what we're about here before you go changing the world, Miss Abigail.'

Abigail stared at the wooded panels and realised her life would never be the same again.

★ ★ ★

Joshua left Molly sleeping on the bed. When he had returned to the room she was lying on top of the covers, wrapped in the blanket. She did not wake so he did not tell her about Drab's appearance. This morning he had a further problem. The man would return before the London coach left. So how was he to leave the inn with the young woman unseen? He decided to take a walk. See if there was any sign of Drab and think.

*   *   *

Abigail did not appreciate being left for nearly half an hour. The long case clock ticked each slow moment as it passed by. And with each, Abigail became more restless. The smell of the polished leather seating hung heavily in the air reminding her of the stagecoach journey. When the door finally opened again, Abigail automatically stood up. A rotund figure of a man dressed in a fashionable style of a coat cut at the waist, which would have been better suited to a man of greater height and straighter posture, greeted her.

'My dear Miss Hammond, whatever brings you all this way, and on your own too. Where is your dear brother, Mr Frederick? He must surely know of your whereabouts, does he not? Has he not already left to be with you and your poor father? I do hope his health improves, I heard he was quite weak. Come with me please. Excuse my manners, I shall send for refreshments then we shall talk.'

Mr Ashton led Abigail, guiding her gently by her elbow towards the room next door. She looked to Martha who was standing staring out into the street.

'Martha, do not stand there day-dreaming. Come now, pay attention!'

'Yes, Miss Hammond, sorry, miss.'

Mr Ashton gave no protest as the woman obediently followed on. He sat Abigail down on a settee and stood before her. 'Now what is it that you have for me?'

With some apprehension Abigail handed the letter to him. Martha stood by the door watching on.

Mr Ashton scratched his balding head and tutted loudly. 'Your father wishes me to draw up certain papers regarding your . . . birthright, and . . . ' He smiled at her. 'However, he wrote this some two years ago but has never seen to it being fulfilled. How very strange, one wonders why ever not.' He glanced at Abigail in a peculiar manner that made her feel very uneasy.

'He is ill, Mr Ashton. He asks that you visit Beckton Manor immediately with a trusted and reliably independent doctor. He is under Mr Frederick's control and lays ill abed, not able to do his own bidding. I am greatly concerned for him and his future well-being.'

'As well you should be, my dear child. Of course Mr Frederick is seeing to his affairs'

She discreetly turned away as she stood up to speak. 'I beseech you. Please do as my father asks, sir. He has seen Frederick in his true light. He gloats over Father and myself and seeks to marry me off to a strange man and . . .'

'Calm yourself, my dear child. All shall be handled well. You are going though a traumatic time. Life changes as we all do — Ecclesiastes 3, there is a time for everything and . . .'

Abigail looked down. This man was one of Frederick's friends. She realised that her cause was totally lost. Her heart felt heavy with worry for her poor father but what could she do? 'Mr Ashton, will you do as Father asks?'

'Why, of course I must. Everything shall be done right and proper. I have a visitor awaiting me in my office, and shall be only a few moments.'

There was a knock on the door.

'Yes, yes, enter.'

A tray was brought on which a silver teapot and china cups had been carefully placed.

'Ah, there you are, my dear. You have a rest and I shall be back before you know I've even gone away.' He muttered something to himself and disappeared with the letter in his hand.

Abigail looked to Martha whose ear was firmly against the door. She put her hand up to stop Abigail speaking for a moment. When Abigail saw Martha gritting her teeth and shaking her head she knew her worst suspicions had been correct.

Martha hurried over to her as she heard the outside door open and shut.

'He's sending word to Frederick,' Martha whispered.

'Quickly, we shall have to go.'

Martha turned to open the door Ashton had left through, but Abigail could hear voices outside.

'This way!' They retraced their steps back to the first waiting room then, as swiftly as they could, slipped out of the room and exited to the street. 'We must collect our baggage and leave this instant,' Martha stated as they both hurried along the street back to the Phoenix Inn.

8

Joshua returned to the Phoenix Inn. He opened the narrow low door and entered the smoky gloom of the tavern. The air was thick with the smell of burning cheap tallow fat candles, ale and the smoke from many a clay pipe. It was a habit he had never liked.

Molly was up and sitting on the chair hugging her bundle. He gave her a plate with ham and bread on it, and a tankard of milk. 'Have this. I need to explain something to you. Drab was here last night looking for you.'

The girl nearly dropped the plate. He held it firmly in his own hand.

'I sent him away. He doesn't know you are here. I aim to get you away. However, it will not be easy. You must trust me and I must delay my journey. It would appear we are to have a little adventure.'

'He'll skin me, mister, if he catches me.'

'I don't doubt it. So we had better stay one step ahead. I want you to wear these. He dropped some clothes at her feet. They were the clothes of a boy.

'You want me to wear breeches?'

'Yes. I want you to wear breeches, shirt, jacket and cap. I want you to leave your old rags here in that fire and I want you to act as though you belong with me. Follow at my side. God knows why, but it appears I am going to help you.'

She felt the quality of the garments and looked up at him and grinned. 'You is a real gent.'

'Say it often enough and I might start believing my own virtues.'

★   ★   ★

Abigail and Martha did not stop until they were well away from the offices of Mr Ashton. They had seen the tall clerk, dressed in black, run out onto the street shouting at two boy runners to look for them, so like hunted animals they had ducked down the narrow snickets and made for the huge gothic cathedral. There they hid within its grandeur to catch their breath. Abigail looked up at the huge arches and highly coloured windows. The light stone, so beautiful in its structure, took her breath away; magnificent, she thought. Abigail wished she could stay there, safe until her life could return to what had previously been her normality. But in her heart she knew that could never be.

'Martha, we have to find a way out of here,' Abigail said, but was also thinking about how to throw the hounds off their scent and buy them some much needed time.

'We could try the door.' Martha pointed to the huge main entrance.

'Come with me.' Abigail ignored her tone and walked boldly up to a member of the cathedral staff, dressed in his black cassock. 'Excuse me, but could you tell me where I might purchase a ticket on a stagecoach destined to London?'

The man smiled at her politely. 'The London coach will leave from the Castle Tavern at midday.' He bowed politely at her.

'Thank you, sir.' She turned to a slightly bemused Martha. 'Come, woman,' Abigail ordered and boldly strolled down the central aisle of the cathedral for all to see. Martha followed behind with their heavy bag.

Once near the main doors, Abigail took the bag from her and skirted around the outside of the building to the Tudor buildings that nestled behind it.

'So what was that charade about?' Martha asked.

'Exactly that, a pretence, I want to give the impression that we are going to London.' Abigail paused outside a dressmaker's shop.

'Could you not let me know what you're doing before you go flouncing off like that? You had my heart in a twirl.'

'A lady would not consult her maid on such issues — you would be expected to follow.' Abigail looked inside the shop and decided it would do.

'Oh would she?'

'Yes, now open the door and do not make a spectacle of yourself.'

Martha flung wide the door and Abigail could hear the woman's deep breath as she stifled her words.

'Can I help you, milady?' A tall straight figure greeted Abigail somewhat apprehensively when Martha entered behind her, panting slightly as she carried their bag.

'Yes, I require a mourning dress, pelisse, hat and gloves.' Abigail held herself straight with complete confidence and decorum.

The woman's eyes lit up at the prospect of the forthcoming sale. 'If you would care to come through to my pattern room I will measure milady and then she can choose her fabrics and patterns.'

'That would be most enjoyable. However, unfortunately I require them today.' Abigail saw the smile drop from the woman's face as she turned to look back at her.

'Today?' she queried. 'This is really quite irregular.'

'Yes, today.' Abigail stared directly at her, not flinching in her resolve.

'Isn't that rather sudden?' The lady tilted her head slightly at her as she spoke.

'Death often is. I am leaving York today and need suitable travelling attire.' Abigail had seen the woman's samples displayed in her pattern room. One, a long black pelisse, would do her fine. If only she could convince the woman to part with it.

'I do not have clothes made ready to wear. I am a perfectionist, ma'am. I make garments of quality that fit my ladies perfectly, so that when their friends and relatives espy them, they all wish to purchase their attire here, from me personally.' She held her fingers together in front of her own exquisite gown. 'There is an establishment that sells second-hand garments of dubious quality, at a reasonable price, near the Barr. Perhaps madam should try there.'

'How much would that 'perfect' pelisse cost?' Abigail asked, gesturing to the back room, and ignoring the slight that had been intended.

'That is one of my most precious show pieces. I could not possibly let anything leave my shop that was not a perfect fit on the person who is seen wearing it.'

'Then you have just missed the opportunity to make a 'cash' sale, madam. Come, Martha, we shall go elsewhere.' Abigail turned to leave, hoping the word 'cash' was sufficient to persuade the woman to part with the pelisse. Abigail knew that many respectable society ladies would pay on account or by note. Some never paid at all, but Abigail could tell by the woman's shrewd eyes that she was an astute business woman.

'Perhaps I could be persuaded to part with such a precious garment if indeed it did fit you adequately.' She disappeared into the back room. Abigail followed. A chaise longue had pride of place along the centre of the wall; its golden chintz gave the room an air of luxury. Two matching chairs were positioned either side of it.

Abigail removed her pelisse and wrapped herself in the black one; it was indeed well made, with a fine silk lining and fur trim. It fitted her comfortably, perhaps a little more room than she needed, but not so much that anyone would notice.

'I will buy it if you ask a fair price.' Abigail stared pointedly at the woman who discreetly licked her lips. Martha was watching her closely. 'Perhaps a little more than your normal charge for the inconvenience I have caused you.'

'I shall charge you the price as I would for the garment to be made up, plus one tenth of the cost as I will not have it to show my customers until I can replace it. Would you consider that fair?'

Martha opened her mouth to speak.

'Have you sold a garment such as this to anyone else recently?' Abigail asked.

The lady smiled and walked over to a desk in the corner. She removed a ledger and opened the leather-bound book, flicking purposefully through its pages.

'I have no need nor wish to extort money from my customers. I do not know what your circumstances are, but you obviously are in a hurry so I shall show you the last sale of the coat. Pay your money and be on your way. I have an important lady arriving shortly to order her new wardrobe and I will give her my complete and utter attention. So here,' she pointed to the figures in her ledger, 'do we have a sale?'

'Yes, we do.' Abigail smiled gratefully. She opened her reticule and started to count out her money. It felt very strange to be handling money herself.

The lady brought over a matching

box hat and a pair of black kid gloves.

'You will need these also, I think.'

'Yes, of course, thank you. I wish to keep the pelisse on.' Abigail pulled off her own gloves and Martha helped to fix the hat on her lady's head.

'Excuse me, my dear, it is worn so.' The lady adjusted Abigail's hat and gave Martha a scathing look.

'Are you staying in York?' she asked idly.

'No, we are making our way to London,' Abigail answered and saw that Martha approved of her lie.

'Well, my dear, you should be fine in this but please go straight to a ladies' outfitter of note, or else no one worth knowing will wish to associate with you.'

Her own coat was wrapped by a young assistant as a large coach drew up outside the establishment.

Instantly, the place was a hive of activity. Two young girls, immaculately dressed with starched white aprons, opened the shop doors wide. A footman was dropping the step of the bright yellow carriage, dramatic against the black trimmings. Abigail stared at the coach. The coat of arms was not one she recognised but it brought back to her memories of her home, Lord Hammond and their own fine livery.

The lady who stepped out was in her middle years, Abigail guessed, but she was exquisitely turned out. Her skin was fair, unlike Abigail's darker hue, her hair like gold and, as she turned to enter the establishment, her green eyes sought out the fawning shop owner. The lady held her head high and erect. Abigail thought this was a woman who knew the value and effect of her own beauty.

'Lady Fenton Grange, I have a tray prepared for you, milady. I hope your journey wasn't too arduous?' The shopkeeper did indeed fawn with all her attention.

'Yes it was. It always is. However, you may show me what you have prepared and I do hope this will not be a wasted journey. I am on my way to see Lord Fenton Grange and need my wardrobe packing today! Should anything be incomplete I shall be left without, and that will not do! When we are back at Over Bagby Hall I shall send my carriage for you again, but now we are on our way to Dower House and I need and demand everything to be perfect, Miss Blossom.'

'Of course, nothing less will do in my establishment.' Miss Blossom looked directly at Abigail who had been waiting to leave.

'Is this to be a public viewing, Blossom?' Lady Fenton Grange glared at Abigail, then stepped in front of her, peering down upon her face. Her green eyes looked full of surprise. 'Do I know you, girl?'

Abigail did not care for her tone or being referred to as a 'girl' once more. She ignored her question and addressed Miss Blossom instead.

'Thank you for your help, Miss Blossom. I shall pass on my approval of your establishment to all my friends.' Abigail saw the older woman grin quickly at her. Abigail turned to summon Martha. She looked to one side of her and then the other to discover Martha had already left the premises.

'Good day,' Abigail said to Miss Blossom, then looked directly at the irate emerald eyes that glared at her. 'No, I don't believe we have met, or are likely to again.' Abigail stepped outside without waiting for the indignant woman's response, although she pitied Miss Blossom who would no doubt receive the wrong side of the woman's tongue. Abigail still felt as though she was being watched by the lady, but she refused to look back at her. Abigail peered up and down the street and then heard a low whistle. It was Martha standing on a corner further down the road from the shop.

'Why on earth did you leave like that?' Abigail was most annoyed. She had not even seen her slip out of the shop. 'I thought we were to stay together.'

Martha shifted uneasily and struggled to balance both the bag and the wrapped parcel. 'Sorry, but I found out where the Whitby coach goes from, but it ain't goin' today.'

'What? We have to go today or else we'll be discovered.' Abigail sighed heavily as she looked up towards the imposing towers of the Minster. 'God, tell me what are we to do now?' she muttered to herself.

'We shall go to ask about hiring a chaise, as the mail coach goes tonight. I think that may be too late.' Martha patted Abigail's arm. 'We have no choice, Mrs Moor. God willing, our future will be protected and safe.'

'Martha, you are . . . '

'Standing here wasting our precious time with this chatter. Now, I have directions to go to a place where we can rent one. It's two streets down to the right, next to the coppersmith's place. So we best be on our way.'

133

'You are a marvel and I'd be lost without you.' Abigail completed her sentence as they walked on.

'So long as you remember that, Mrs Moor.'

9

Joshua and a boy left the inn. They made their way around the huge Minster that dominated the sky line and headed towards Micklegate. Here they had been told they would be able to rent a small chaise. Joshua walked as casually as he could with a slight limp. Molly walked confidently by his side. The big cap shaded her face. The clothes were roomy on her but warm and comfortable. Joshua glanced down at her with amusement as she had her back straight and had adopted a much bolder gait. She played the part well.

They crossed the soiled and muddied street to the yard where he could see a coach and gig housed.

'This is the place.' Joshua moved his bag from one hand to the other and placed a hand on Molly's shoulder. 'Keep that hat tilted down and let me do the talking. Whatever happens, if you see Drab, don't run. Stay at my side.'

'Yes, guv.' Her voice was deeper than usual.

'Sir, you've not fallen out of the Dial's'

'Where?'

'Just stay quiet.'

★　★　★

Abigail approached the yard. Martha had done well to find this place. They would soon be on their way. Within moments she had been given the choice of a gig, which neither of them could possibly handle, or the expense of renting a coach.

She could afford it but Martha was dead set against it. Her maid wanted to keep as much money back as possible for their survival in Whitby. Undecided, she was surprised to find that she had competition for the vehicle. The gentleman and a boy were also interested in it.

'Martha we shall have to take it or we shall be discovered.' Abigail stood forward.

'Sir, we are already in discussions for the purchase of the coach to take us over to Whitby.'

The owner's eyes almost sparkled; Abigail presumed at his delight that he could obtain an extortionate fee from the highest bidder.

'Whitby,' the gentleman repeated and looked down at the boy. 'This coach will seat all of us comfortably. Could I suggest we share it?'

The owner looked slightly puzzled. 'I thought you were heading south, sir.'

'Indeed, but I should like to show the boy the sea first.'

Martha nudged Abigail. 'Very well, how soon can we leave?'

The owner told them it would be ready within half an hour which seemed to please all concerned.

★　★　★

Joshua and Molly stood by the coach, whilst Abigail and Martha were seated in a small waiting room.

'Where did he find the boy, Martha? I thought he was with a young girl.'

'After you retired last night a man came looking for a young lass. He didn't look kindly, in fact the opposite. Your young gentleman was very noble again. He stopped the man from finding her. I reckon he's some sort of guardian angel. He limps.'

Abigail blushed. 'I hadn't noticed,' she answered casually.

'You never were any good at lying Abigail.'

'You really do underestimate me, Martha,' Abigail answered and waited in silence until the postilion took up his position.

★　★　★

Abigail sat opposite the gentleman, whilst Martha happily seated herself opposite the 'boy'. At first Abigail stared out of the carriage window at a group of raggedy children playing with a stick and stone in the first village that they passed through. The poverty that she saw touched her deeply. 'What has happened here?' Abigail asked. 'Why are they so poor?'

'Nothing and everything happened at the same time,' Joshua explained. 'Not one single thing did this to them, but several over the last few years.'

'You are not making any sense, sir.' Abigail could see a look of sadness on his face but she did not understand the implications of the words.

'It does not make sense to them either. That's the problem. They work hard yet bad weather has meant poor crops, little food and menfolk lost to Napoleon in the war or returning home bashed in body and mind, or both, and workless; all that came together meaning people are poor and food is scarce.'

Martha looked at Abigail and shrugged. 'Their world is far removed from yours, Miss Abigail, and for that you should give hearty thanks.'

'But what about the parish funds? Father always contributes most generously. The poor are always given their share of charity, are they not?' Abigail had heard Reverend Hardiman say as much on one of his visits, usually when he was asking for her father to help support some event or other.

'Does he?' Martha shook her head and Abigail did not like the attitude of her maid. 'It's just not enough.'

Abigail did not like the hard tone of her voice. Her words almost came out with an accusation of some kind thinly hidden behind them.

Martha took hold of Abigail's arm as she reached for some coins in her purse. 'Now, lass, what are you going to do with those?'

'Throw them to the children, so their mothers can buy them food.' Abigail thought it was the least she could do. If the parish was not coping with its poor then anything would be of help to them, and gratefully received, she reasoned. Martha prevented Abigail from carrying out her gesture.

'We will need all that you have. Don't you see that we could also end up like them poor children in the street? If we can't find suitable accommodation and work for the both of us, we could starve ourselves.'

Abigail was appalled. 'How dare you speak to me in this manner and in front of strangers too!'

'My name is Mr Joshua Rusk, until six months ago a captain in the Rifles. Now we are not strangers. I think your maid is quite correct and very observant.'

Molly looked up. Joshua removed the girl's cap and she smiled at Martha.

'Well my maid speaks nonsense! We will send the militia from Whitby to rescue Father and all will be as it was.' Abigail was not prepared for Martha's outspoken response.

'Just like that? So, having found out that your own father's 'good' friend, Mr Ashton, would prefer to believe in

Mr Frederick's word rather than yours, you honestly believe the militia will take your word on the matter without proof or question? Don't you see, Abigail, you will certainly be seen as no more than a trouble-maker out to feather her own nest? They will not, nor care why you should not consider obeying Mr Frederick and marrying that bag of trouble, Hackman. He has position and money.'

'He employs Drab!' Molly stated.

'Small world we live in ladies.'

'Mr Ashton may have doubted my motives because he is such a good friend of the family. After all, I was a total stranger to him. That does not mean that the militia officers would do likewise. You cannot be sure they would doubt my honesty, integrity or credibility.' Abigail saw that her servant was totally unconvinced as in fact she herself was, but she had to try to believe they had a future, that all would be well. She had now seen real poverty for the first time in her life and she did not like its look or smell.

'Don't you think they may just be a little pre-occupied with their own problems, overseeing a busy port and trying to stop the trade around here — or at least trying to do something to stop them? There is no going back, Abigail, unless your father makes a full recovery and returns to his previous good health, which is doubtful, I'm sorry to say.' Martha squeezed Abigail's hand gently. 'You and I have to make a new life for ourselves — one that will involve working to keep a roof over our heads.'

Abigail saw the panic in Martha's face. The whole adventure to her was exciting, liberating and a means to an end — escaping Frederick's despicable plans for her. However, Martha knew the reality of life and their prospects to her were obviously daunting. Abigail would not give in to such thoughts. They would survive and succeed.

'What trade?' Abigail asked naively.

'Smuggling, contraband, it's a thriving business around those parts,'

Martha explained and Joshua nodded.

'You heard this from Ezekiel?' Abigail asked.

Martha lifted her eyes slowly to meet Abigail's. 'You be careful what you're saying about my Ezekiel. He's a good man and honest too.'

'Oh, cheer up, Martha. Look on it as a challenge, a chance to see the sea.' Abigail tried to lift the conversation and inject some kind of hope into the conversation.

She looked at the gentleman and the girl. 'You, too, are on an adventure, are you not?'

'You'll excuse me if I don't quite share your enthusiasm, miss.' Martha's reply was terse, but the girl's eyes were full of life and mischief.

'Honestly, Martha, sometimes I think you have no faith.' Abigail's retort caused her maidservant to take in a sharp breath, then burst into a fit of laughter.

'You amaze me.' Martha wiped a tear away from her eye as her laugh subdued to a chuckle. 'It is easy to have faith when all your creature comforts are met, and your bed is dry and comfortable. Let's see how far it goes when your room smells of the damp and the bugs bite you in your sleep — if you can get any, that is!'

'So, are you saying that only the rich can afford to have a faith and that all others must live in despair?' Abigail rounded on Martha.

'No, I'm not saying that either! Cheeky little . . . ' Martha flushed as she looked up at Joshua who appeared to be amused by their disagreement.

Abigail stared at her flustered maid. She had cracked through her normally capable exterior and hit a raw nerve.

'Look, save that sort of thinking for folks who have time to dwell on such things. What I'm trying to tell you, 'Miss' Abigail, is that we have to look out for ourselves, our own future, in case things don't go right with your father. That's all I'm saying. It's a cruel world out there, and now we are a part of it.'

'What you really mean is that I am a stupid spoilt child who has been sheltered too long. To some extent I always have been. But I shall learn, Martha. I am intelligent, and I am far from weak.' Abigail saw her maidservant smile, then pat her knee as if comforting the young child she once was.

'Aye — that you are, lass. So if we get into trouble you can think your way out of it, whilst I get a job that pays us money to buy our victuals.'

Joshua laughed, whilst Martha looked out of the window, and Abigail guessed she was smirking.

'If it comes to that — 'if', it does — then I shall find suitable work also. I shall not sit back and idle whilst you labour.' Abigail was annoyed when Martha did not acknowledge, what to her, was a magnanimous gesture. After all, she had never expected to become a servant. She was raised as a lady.

'You knew my mother, Martha. You knew who she was and I need to be told the truth.' Abigail saw that her quick turn of conversation had caught Martha off guard. The woman blustered for a moment or two then grinned at herself and at her own behaviour.

'I shall tell you what I can, Miss Abigail, and no more. So accept this and, for your own sake, don't question me any further, for there are some things a person is better off not knowing.' Martha waited a few moments for her to agree. 'Now is not the place.'

Abigail looked at their fellow travellers, the girl's eyes wide hanging on their every word, the gentleman meeting her stare.

'It's my right to be told the truth — my birthright.' Abigail saw Martha look out of the window over the vale, not saying a word. 'Sir, I must entrust you as you must us. This girl — I take it you are not kidnapping her, but rescuing her in some way.'

'Yes, I am saving her from a fate that many a vulnerable young woman has befallen.'

'Why?' Martha asked.

'Martha!'

'No, it is a fair question. Because of the children in the village back there, because of the dead fathers, brothers, uncles and lovers who do not return to look after their children. Or because a bullet in my leg turned my brain soft.'

'Then let us help each other,' Abigail said.

Joshua nodded.

The landscape would soon change as they ascended from the vale of York by the steep road to the open moor that would lead them to the coast.

'Martha, tell me what you can and, for now, it will have to do.' Abigail watched Martha swallow slightly and she realised that whatever her past involved it was something that touched Martha deeply too.

'Your mother was a governess at a large hall.' The coach jolted as they reached the steep bank. The post chaise rattled as it was pulled upwards. Abigail thought it exciting, but Martha held onto the seat for dear life. She was scared.

'Where? Which hall?' Abigail asked eagerly, desperate to know anything about her mother.

'No questions,' Martha said, still distracted by the views as they climbed higher. 'I will tell you only the details that won't cause you too much pain to know. The hall was bigger than Beckton Manor. It was grand, fit for a king. She had been, I believe, the youngest daughter of a wealthy family . . . '

'What was her name, Martha?' Abigail asked, again eager to know anything that brought this shadowy figure of her mother closer to her. She buried her hands deeply into her muff, holding them tightly as she hung on every word Martha uttered.

'Grace, her name was Grace and it suited her very well because she was filled with it, in every sense of the word . . . ' Martha looked fondly at her and Abigail understood how much her maid, her own friend, had loved her mother.

Martha's face filled with a joy that was infectious as she remembered her dear friend Grace.

'What was her surname? Perhaps I can trace my true family?' Abigail said excitedly.

'No! You must never do that for it would only bring you shame and pain. They turned their back on Grace and disowned her leaving her to a life of solitude and to her fate. That — her fate, I mean, was one that no young woman should have to face on her own, especially a lady who was well-bred. She was bright as a polished brass button, intelligent, always reading books in the library.' Martha grinned to herself. 'She would have been better than Frederick, for sure, at his law work . . . but she was a lady and not a gentleman. Good for marriage . . . '

'So what did fate do to her?' Abigail asked, whilst bracing herself for the unpleasant truth.

Martha looked at her with slightly watery eyes. 'My dear, Miss Abigail, the answer is simple and hard because it is . . . you.'

Abigail looked horrified, an empty sinking feeling threatening to engulf her. 'What do you mean . . . me?'

'You should have been her greatest blessing, but she was single and you were not born from the seed of love. She was never married.'

'Was she rap . . . ' She saw the concern in Joshua's eyes. This conversation had turned more personal than ever she could have imagined. 'You know what I mean, was she taken against her will?' Abigail felt almost sick at the thought. Not only for her mother's horrific experience, but that Frederick was even more correct in his description of her as a 'bastard' than she would have ever liked to accept. Up to this point his words had been no more than empty weapons said purely to inflict pain, but they had never really hit her hard because she had not believed there was any truth in them. She presumed that poverty had led her to be abandoned by her parents to an almshouse, not by a defiled mother.

'No, she wasn't, not in the way you mean . . . '

'How many ways are there?' Abigail asked sharply, and then regretted her abrupt manner.

Martha raised her head and gave her a warning look. 'Miss Abigail! I'll explain as best I can if you'll stop interrupting me like that. I know more about such things than you and your books, dear child.'

'Sorry,' Abigail said quietly, taking the rebuke as it was deserved. She had talked to Hetty about such things and they had gossiped about another servant, Rebecca, and her antics with James the stable lad. Martha did not know everything about her, Abigail thought to herself.

'Grace took pity on the master of the house at a very vulnerable time in his life. She didn't mean to become involved with him in any way. She had a good heart and merely tried to help him through his grief when he lost his son, his only child. Grace had no idea what sort of a man he really was. He was clever, with an ambitious wife, and they desperately wanted an heir. His wife was beautiful but did not conceive one, so in order to protect his fortune and line, yet keep his young wife, she stayed with friends whilst he seduced your mother. She was, as I said, well-bred and educated. She never realised what was happening to her until it was too late; she had no idea of the evil ways of this world. Grace was gentle and naive always looking on the bright side of life. Like you, she thought everything in this world, even the bad things, would have a good side to them. Grace didn't know what Lady . . . what her mistress was capable of. She didn't stand a chance against the two of them. The inevitable happened and she became pregnant. Once pregnant they waited to see if it was a boy, and . . . oh dear, I've already said far too much.' Martha's eyes spilled out silent tears as she relived what was obviously for her a painful and distressing memory.

'They wanted a boy but ended up with a daughter — me.'

Abigail held the woman's arm and bit her lower lip as she quietly resented her own gender more than ever in her life before. It was so unfair. She felt that her own emotions were in turmoil. 'No, Martha, you have not said too much — rather, not enough. Who were these wicked people?'

'That I will never tell you for they would finish you off, one way or another. You on your own are in no position to harm them or their reputation, but they could destroy you as they did your mother. To protect you, that secret will go to the grave with me, so don't waste your breath asking me again. I mean that, Abigail.' Martha stared at her and there was a determination in her eyes that was absolute.

Martha had a defiant look on her face that Abigail had seen many times over the years. It was one that meant there was no use pressing the point. Abigail left it there.

'So what happened to my mother, Martha? Surely I have a right to know that?' Abigail was filled with frustration. There were people living their lives still twenty years after they had destroyed her mother's reputation and it appeared that nobody had brought them to justice.

'She died, love.' Martha could not look at her.

'In childbirth?' Abigail's heart felt as though it would break.

'Afterwards, lass . . . It was not your fault, none of it. Abigail, your mother would have been extremely proud of you and she could not have found you a better home than the one you have shared with Lord Hammond.'

Molly's jaw had dropped. Abigail saw Joshua gently close it with one gloved finger. He looked at Abigail.

'Yes, she could. I could have been with her,' she said.

'Miss, don't live in regret, change your life and embrace the future, whatever it is — you have a life to embrace.'

Abigail was touched by Joshua's

words but was unable to respond. Instead she sat in silence, slowly repeating one word over and over again in her mind — Grace. If ever she was fortunate enough to have a baby girl, conceived and born of love, it would be called Grace. This she promised her dead mother, who for the first time in Abigail's life, had a name and was somehow now very real to her.

Abigail was glad when the post chaise finally neared the coast. She was excited as a child as she had never seen the sea. She peered across the countryside where, in the distance, a grey blue mass of water could be seen. The air was different; it smelt of salt and was fresher. The distant call of gulls was proof that they were nearing their destination. In the far distance she could see the ruins of an old abbey standing majestically on the headland.

'Look, look!' Molly was tugging at Martha's skirt.

'Yes, I see it.' Martha's voice was flat, with absolutely no enthusiasm.

Abigail looked at her and could only see gloom in the woman's face.

'What is it? Surely it is good to be back here? Martha, is this your home town?' Abigail stared at her waiting for a reply. At first there wasn't one.

'My Tobias died when I was only newly wed. He was a fisherman and there was an awful storm. I was so pleased to leave this place and thought I never need come back here again. It has brought me nothing but bad luck. I fear nothing has changed. It's not a place where I want to be for long.'

'I'm sorry about your Tobias, Martha. I never knew you were married. But then there is so much I have never been told, that I need to know. I'm sure that once you have returned and faced your pain it will no longer be so great.' Abigail squeezed Martha's hand.

Martha pulled it away from her. 'You're only a child. You have no idea. The pain is always there, it never goes away. Now, I have to live with it again, night and day. I am supposed to look on that treacherous sea and see what? Beauty or the murderous destroyer of maidens' hearts? There is evil here. It feeds on the sick, the poor and those who grieve, and you who know nothing tell me what it will be like. God help us!' Martha snuffled.

'Yes, if we ask Him, I'm sure he will. There is evil everywhere; here the sea claims lives; at the manor Frederick would claim ours. We have no choice, but at least here you know the place, the past and the dangers. Together we can survive, just don't give in to this maudlin spirit of gloom, Martha. Be strong, I am.' Abigail watched as Martha stared at her almost in disbelief, as if seeing her anew.

'Yes, by God. I believe you are. But Abigail, you have no idea of what lies ahead of us, only what lies behind. You have led a cherished life.'

'Yes, Martha, I do know. The future lies ahead and at this present moment it seems a lot clearer than my past.'

She saw Joshua smile.

10

The chaise pulled up in front of a large hotel opposite the harbour's side. Abigail was filled with excitement; mirrored in the eyes of Molly. She entered the vibrant bustling port in awe. New buildings were being added to the west side, whilst the older town on the east side was a huddle of houses clinging to the steep side of the headland. Red pantiled roofs appearing higgledy piggledy were overlooked by an old church and the abbey's stark ruins. The two halves of this busy whaling port were joined together by a wooden swing bridge.

The sea crashed and roared, the gulls kwaarked noisily overhead. Fishermen tended their boats, women and children did a myriad of chores and all seemed to be a swirl of activity. Abigail alighted from the coach and breathed the fresh bracing air. No one paid them any attention as vendors hustled with fishermen and passengers alike. Martha stepped down and shivered. Her shoulders were rounded, her whole persona drooped with a defeated air, and she seemed barely able to look at the harbour side. Instead, she waited whilst two leather bags were placed on the ground in front of them. Martha pulled at one and was about to say something to the driver when Abigail stopped her and spoke boldly to the man.

'Thank you for a comfortable journey.' Before she could offer him a coin Joshua stepped in and tipped him.

'Thank you, sir,' he answered cheerfully, pocketing it quickly, obviously pleased with his generosity.

Once inside the inn Abigail stared at the entrance, she sipped the tea they had ordered and waited patiently for their meal to be brought to them.

'What do you think you are playing at?' Martha asked quietly. 'We are supposed to be losing ourselves in this awful place, not sitting in public.'

'Mind your language please, Martha.' Abigail saw her tense, she looked up at the ceiling with an attitude of despair.

'May I suggest that we eat and then you take young Molly with you for a breath of fresh air. Find her some decent clothes, if possible, and seek your relative with whom you wish to live. I would like to talk to your mistress.' Joshua seemed to have Martha's approval, as she nodded.

'Well, what better way to lose yourself, Martha, than in a good cause.'

'Lady Fenton-Grange. If you come straight through we will have your favourite meal served forthwith.' The hotel owner greeted the lady who had alighted from her fine coach. He was almost bowing as he took each step. She had such bearing and confidence, that Abigail was quite lost in admiration.

'I would have thought that I would be allowed to refresh myself first. I am most fatigued by the horrendous journey. I do not enjoy carriages or

horses,' the lady snapped back ungrate-
fully.

'Yes, yes of course, milady. Whenever
you wish it, it shall be ready.' A door
was opened and the lady and her two
maids passed through the lounge
unaware of Abigail's presence.

'Martha, did you . . . ' Abigail turned
to see Martha re-emerging from where
she had bent down beneath the table.

'What are you doing?' Abigail watched
her face re-appear, ruddy from bending.

Martha looked sheepishly back at her
as she seated herself at the table and
held up a spoon. 'I dropped it on the
floor,' she said as an explanation.

Abigail looked at her suspiciously.
'Well try not to be so clumsy. Did you
see who that was?'

'Who what was, miss?' Martha
looked blankly around the inn.

'Your food, ma'am.' The waiter placed
their plates down in front of them and
Martha was instantly all enthusiasm for
it, her eyes focussed wholly on what she
was doing. 'I was getting so hungry that

I was starting to think I'd faint for lack of victuals.'

Joshua was watching both women carefully but Molly only had eyes for the food.

'Sorry, Miss Abigail. I told you, me and Whitby have a past and it made me clumsy like.'

'What absolute nonsense. You really are full of superstitious humbug. You missed that lady who arrived at Miss Blossom's shop before we left York. She has come here too,' Abigail informed her. 'And Martha, please remember I am Mrs Moor now, a young widow.'

'Small world, isn't it? Still we won't be mixing in the same circles as that one, so no good getting all friendly with her.' Martha ate with enthusiasm.

'I don't think anyone can get too 'friendly' with one such as her. She is far too grand.' Abigail thought about her for a moment; she was a woman who knew her place, aloof and above all others, unlike Abigail who was all adrift.

It was not long before Joshua and Abigail were left alone. She felt a little nervous but tried hard not to show it.

'How do you know Lady Fenton Grange, Miss . . . Mrs Moor, and do you intend to keep your new persona indefinitely?'

'I don't but our paths crossed and she seemed to think she had met me before. She's beautiful, isn't she?'

'In a worldly sense, yes, but not in an attractive way.'

'How do you differentiate?'

'Easily, she has an external beauty whilst inner beauty shines through from a person's core.' He was looking at her in a very curious way, as if studying her features.

She blushed slightly. 'What will you do now?'

'I should like to ask you for help with young Molly. She is escaping the clutches of a brute and needs a family.'

'I am also escaping, sir.'

'So, escape together. Stay in a safe place whilst I try and find out what is happening with your father. I can travel freely. If I return to Beckton Manor and speak with him, I will be better placed to help you than anyone.'

'Why would you go to so much trouble?'

He leaned back in his chair and sipped his wine. 'Because, at the moment I have little else to do than to help damsels in distress, and besides, I love a good mystery, and you 'Mrs Moor', have provided me with one.'

★ ★ ★

'You look all flushed, Miss Abigail,' Martha exclaimed quietly as she bent over averting her eyes from that of her young mistress. She picked up their bag. Martha bracing herself against a strong gust of cold salty air that blew in from the sea and up the River Esk.

Joshua and Molly were talking quietly, still near the inn. The girl looked perplexed, unsure in some way, but she placed her hand in his and he walked her over to Abigail.

'It's the sea air, Martha,' Abigail commented as she watched them. 'And please remember, that I am now Mrs Moor.'

'There is something you should know, Martha. I have agreed to help young Molly.'

'How can you help anyone when you can't help yourself?' Martha snapped. 'I'm thinking it's not the air that's affecting you but someone's handsome face and dark locks.'

'Martha you speak out of turn,' Abigail rebuked.

'No, lass, I speak out of experience.' Martha grinned back at her, brimming with confidence.

Abigail knew the woman was quite right in her assumption. She could not help but let a little smile turn her lips upwards at the corners.

'Did you find accommodation, Napp?' he asked.

'Aye, for us, but listen up, we can't take on waifs and strays.'

Molly looked downcast.

Martha added, 'Beyond this scrap, but there is no room for thee.'

'That won't be necessary I won't be staying. I shall pay you for the girl's keep until she is found work.'

Abigail was going to dismiss the gesture as unnecessary, but Martha accepted his offer saying how they too had their problems. Abigail looked away.

'Come on, we need to go down here.' Martha led the way along a sweeping cobbled road. This led to a narrow pathway between two buildings. The alley bent right then left and narrowed. Abigail didn't like it at all. It was dark, and confining. The doors to ramshackle homes led directly onto it. She couldn't help herself imagining one opening and being bodily dragged inside never to be seen again. Gratefully, Abigail stepped out onto another broader cobbled street, filled with more people bustling around, busy with their livelihoods.

Abigail looked at the tall inn ahead of them and the coach yard next to it. The building was narrow. The two low beamed windows were separated by a green door. 'Won't it be rather noisy here?' Abigail asked, somewhat apprehensively.

'Ha! Lass, we haven't taken rooms at a hotel. We have to make your money last. No, we go down here.'

Abigail looked anxiously at Joshua who placed a reassuring hand on her shoulder leading her forward.

'Take this as a temporary residence. Once I have made my enquiries I shall find more suitable accommodation, for now, you need to keep low and hide away.'

'If you speak to Father then all will be as it should be again and I shall return to Beckton,' Abigail said with little optimism.

Martha cut across the street, turning left and walking down toward the noisy harbour, but then slipped through into another snicket between the buildings to a small yard. To the right was a high wall that was the other side of the inn and, to the left, a long low building with smoke billowing from a chimney stack that was part of the building facing them. It appeared to be the back of a bakers' shop and the low building was the bakery itself. The smell of fresh bread made Abigail feel quite homesick for Mrs Giles's tasty cakes at the manor house. Across the road from them was the laundry.

'We have a room up there above the bakers'. Cosy or what, eh? Martha has done real good this time, hasn't she?' Martha hesitated a moment, but if it was for a few words of praise it was a moment lost. Abigail just stared at the ramshackle buildings, so the woman continued, 'I didn't think this place would still be running but Biddy is still going strong and her cakes and bread are the best in the whole of Yorkshire.'

Abigail liked the aroma of food and the warmth the building exuded. She patted Martha's shoulder in a rare moment of appreciation of her maid. It was the first time the woman had really looked relaxed since returning to Whitby and Abigail hoped it was a good sign that things would be happier here, if not easy. 'You have done very well, Martha. Is Biddy the owner?'

'Yes, I works Monday to Saturday and has Sundays off, as I'm family,' Martha said proudly. 'Biddy's me sister-in-law, always did get on, we did, then lost touch when I had to leave so sudden like. Mister, you and Molly wait here as I need to talk to Biddy about the lass.'

She side-glanced at Abigail then quickly picked up the bag and made her way up the rickety stairs as if she'd said something wrong again.

'When do I work, Martha?' Abigail asked, but was greeted by a derisory look.

'You get yourself settled in, lass. You have a lot of changes to make first. Then we'll see how things go on.'

Martha opened the door to a room. It was certainly warm and the strange uneven wooden floor gave it a certain character. The walls were plain plaster and had little adornment. A large pewter plate hung on a chimney breast and a besom was propped up in the corner. A few scattered clip rugs were thrown haphazardly on the floor which gave the room a more homely feel. The four-poster bed, laden with old quilted blankets over its feathered mattress was placed against the west wall facing the window that looked out over the ramshackle tiled roofs. Two chairs, a small table and a set of drawers were the only other furniture in the room.

'This is very pleasant, Martha, where is your room?' Abigail asked as she flopped onto the bed.

'Miss, this is my room!' Martha looked at Abigail as if she should have realised.

'Yes, of course.' Abigail turned back towards the door.

'This is 'our' room — we share, Mrs

Moor, no doubt with the young lass too.' Martha stared at her and Abigail realised she should have expected it. For a moment she had forgotten that her new world had just begun in earnest; she would have to sleep with her maid. 'This, miss, is a palace compared to what most put up with . . .'

'Yes,' Abigail laughed, 'but it was worth asking you, just to see the look of dismay on your face. Forgive me for teasing you.' Abigail smiled. 'Now, I'll sleep at this side of the bed and you can sleep there. And the girl will be on a low cot over there. We shall fix one for her. I hope you do not snore too loudly.'

Martha shook her head as if not sure she should believe her jest, but Abigail did not care for she was looking to the window, staring out at a strange land, where a tumultuous sea replaced green fields, and narrow brick houses with pantiled roofs replaced the open spaces of land. She braced herself because she had to adapt to it, and quickly. Then, as her eyes settled on the ruined abbey overlooking them on the high horizon, she felt a jolt as this was the place where her story began and it would be there that Martha would take her back to explain the events of nearly twenty-one years ago to the day.

'Afterwards, when you have introduced me to your 'Biddy' we should take the fresh sea air together and you can show me where it was that I was found.' Abigail looked pointedly at Martha.

'You can take what air you wish, miss, but I've had enough fresh sea air to last me till Christmas; besides, I have news to catch up on with me family, what's left of it . . . '

'At least you have one,' Abigail interjected.

Martha placed her fists squarely on her hips and continued unperturbed, ' . . . and things to do.' Martha did not wait for her reply. 'Now I'm going. Join us when you're ready.'

She left, and Abigail looked at the door momentarily, seething that her maid should dismiss her so. But then her vision settled on Martha's small bag and Abigail wondered . . .

★ ★ ★

Abigail stared at the bag. It was not hers and she should not look within it but then no one was doing or behaving as they should any more. Things were changing all the time and she had to become more independent. She opened the door slightly and stared down the rickety wooden stairs. Abigail tiptoed down half a dozen or so and peered through the top murky square of a window and into the bakery. She saw Martha drinking from a tankard and eating something. She was deep in conversation with a large-framed woman who was relating her news with great animation and enthusiasm. That, Abigail realised, was 'Biddy'. Satisfied that neither woman looked as though they were about to leave for the foreseeable future, she returned to the room and dropped the latch quietly. She carefully opened the strap on Martha's bag and lifted her few garments out, carefully placing them on the rug at the side of the bag in the exact same order in which she removed them. She had, to Abigail's surprise, a few guineas in a purse. Abigail wondered if they came from her father or her friend at the inn. Either way, Martha had never mentioned to her that she had any money of her own.

A small prayer book was wrapped in a silk handkerchief. The embroidered monogram in the corner had been removed, but when Abigail lifted it to the light she thought she could make out the shape of an I or a J. She could not be sure. The prayer book within had been inscribed, *'To my dear and trustworthy friend. My only true one. Grace'*.

Abigail swallowed and stroked it fondly. Would Martha ever share this treasure with her, Grace's own daughter? Time would tell. She placed it back in the silk, folding it in its original creases so it may look undisturbed once more. Abigail wiped her eye with her finger and removed the last garment. There appeared only to be the bottom of the bag. Abigail could not help but feel downhearted as, although she did not know what she was searching for, she had felt something more than a sentimental token may have rested within it. She felt around inside but there were no hidden compartments or pockets so she carefully replaced each item in turn. Once the bag was refastened she turned to the chair where Martha had dropped her muffler and bonnet. Abigail picked them up and threw them onto the bed, then flopped down onto the chair. She was thinking of joining the two women down in the bakery when she saw something that looked like parchment poking out of the muffler.

'Of course!' Abigail exclaimed quietly, and ran over to it. She saw her father's handwriting on the outside. It simply said, 'To Napp'.

Abigail opened it with some trepidation. It seemed very terse — not Martha or Mrs Napp, just Napp. Abigail read on. Her father's handwriting was unsteady, the ink and paper much fresher than the other two letters that had been within the Bible.

You must make sure Abigail has no knowledge of her parentage at whatever cost to you this takes. Your services have been well rewarded over the years. For all my sins she is the one thing in my life that I am proud of. Keep her away from Lady FG and her father. She must have no knowledge that her mother still lives in Ebton. Keep it that way. Collect your coin from Ezekiel.

Abigail stared blankly at it for a moment not able to move. Keep her from Lady FG — Fenton-Grange! For all his sins? What sins? Her mother lives? Where is Ebton? Who is her real father? If Martha will not tell her then her own mother surely would. Her mother was alive! Abigail's heart lifted with joy. Now all she had to do was find her. She sat down on the bed and breathed deeply. Abigail heard movement downstairs and folded the note, quickly placing it back in the pocket within the muffler. She dropped them back on the chair with the bonnet and then flung herself back on the bed, closing her eyes as if asleep when Martha re-entered the room.

'Abigail, wake yourself up a bit, lass. It is time for you to come down and meet Biddy. No use hiding in here.'

Without opening her eyes Abigail answered, 'I'll be down shortly.'

Martha seemed to hesitate. 'You all right, miss?'

'Yes, just thinking. I'll be down in a few moments,' Abigail repeated, waiting until she heard the door close before she moved. Placing her bonnet back on her head and her money within her pocket, she collected her thoughts and her bag. It was time for her to move on.

★　★　★

Abigail watched Molly, Joshua, Martha and Biddy all sitting around a small stove chatting.

Joshua put his hand in his pocket and retrieved some coins. 'Could I possibly leave this for Molly's care?' he asked the baker.

Biddy stepped forwards. Her manner was brusque but not unkind, 'You may. Don't bring anymore.'

He smiled and nodded.

Abigail remembered the elegant and haughty Lady Fenton-Grange. Lady F.G. apparently the woman did know her — there was a connection, but what was it?

'Where does she sleep?' the woman asked.

'With Martha,' Abigail said boldly, as she stepped forwards. Her answer and sudden appearance caused all heads to turn towards her.

'I am glad to make your acquaintance, Biddy, and thank you for accommodating us at such short notice. However . . . ' she glanced at Joshua who held her gaze, 'I will not be staying here,' turning quickly to Biddy she added, ' . . . comfortable as your room is. I too will be travelling to Ebton for a few days or so. I have family there.' She stared defiantly down at Martha. 'Someone I am eager to be reunited with.'

Martha let out a gasp in shock, her composure suddenly very shaky. 'Miss . . . Mrs M . . . '

'There is nothing more to say on the matter, Martha. I have made my own decision.' Abigail glared at Martha. 'Sir, if you would be so kind as to escort me to Ebton. Martha, I shall leave you with your family, whilst I visit mine. Sir, will you be good enough to act as my chaperone?'

'I . . . ' Joshua started to speak. He looked a little lost for words but Abigail gave him the most appealing look she could manage and saw a faint smile appear on his lips. 'I would be honoured,' he added.

'Miss . . . ' Martha began.

'Mrs, Martha, it may not have been for long, but I would have thought you could remember a change of title!' Abigail's words came out sharper than she intended, but they had an instant affect. Martha's cheeks turned a burning red, deeper than those of the baker woman.

'You can't do this. It's sheer folly!' Martha had stepped in front of Abigail but the taller young woman merely stared beyond her.

'My bag is packed, sir,' Abigail pointed to it, 'If you would be so kind . . . '

'Of course.' Joshua collected it, opening the bakers' door as two customers entered.

Abigail tilted her head down to stare into the livid eyes of Martha Napp and said in a quiet voice, 'You lied to me, again. I read my father's note to you. I can do this, Martha, just you watch me!'

'You little fool!' Martha snapped at her in a barely audible whisper.

Without another word she left, following Joshua down the busy street and wondering if she had totally lost leave of her senses.

★   ★   ★

Lord Hammond stared out of his large bay window. His room was central to the house. He was snugly wrapped in warm blankets with a silver tray at his side resting on an inlaid walnut table. He could see the vast expanse of his estate. Lord Hammond had rebuilt the place from the ruin his father's gambling debts had left it in. He was proud of what he had achieved, yet, the methods he had resorted to in order to keep the family estate together he was not particularly proud of. He smiled to himself, though. His own son owned a firm of lawyers too. Life, he mused was strange in the way irony crept in and wove its way throughout it.

There was a knock on the door and Frederick entered, smiling broadly. 'Father, I was informed that you were sufficiently recovered to arise. I am pleased your strength is returning.'

'Frederick, it is a truly pleasant sight to see you smile. What has put you in such good spirits?' Lord Hammond asked as he weakly put his hand out to lift the Wedgewood cup that was upon the silver tray at the side of him. His hand wavered and he nearly spilt the sweet tea. Eventually, he managed to take one sip before he placed it back down onto the tray.

'Your sister would have helped me, Frederick,' he said simply as a rebuke, as the younger man watched him struggle.

'I presume you mean Abigail.' Frederick stared at his father, who shrugged, tired by his continual bickering over Abigail's position within the household. 'Possibly she would have, or her wretched maid, but she is not here, neither of them are here, Father, but I am. They have fled, like thieves in the night. You will not regain strength if you do not use your arm yourself,' Frederick replied bluntly.

'So you do wish me to recover then,

Frederick? I wondered for a while there if my demise would please you.' He stared at the calculative eyes of his son. So like those of his late wife Georgiana, who had been so eager to marry him and his estate. It was such a shame that the baby had died too. Then their own daughter, Abigail, that he should have had, would have been legally and morally Frederick's sister; unlike the pitiful baby that replaced her with the aid of the uncouth Napp woman.

'Of course I do, Father. I don't fear Abigail. I have sent her future husband to find her and fetch her back here. She will be married, very soon. I would like you to see that.'

'He has not asked me for her hand.' Lord Hammond became agitated.

'You have had 'business' dealings with him for years.' Frederick smiled as his father almost fell from his chair, whilst trying to stand — to reach him, to plead with him on Abigail's behalf.

'You don't know what he is like. He is a heartless rogue. Call him back, do you hear me? He shall not have my Abigail. The man's a . . . a . . . '

Watching helplessly, his heir left the room and he cursed his every footstep, and his own foolishness for leaving his final arrangements too late.

* * *

'I think we need to talk, Miss or Mrs Moor. Either here, in a quiet corner somewhere cosy and private or on our journey north; the choice is entirely yours — but talk we will.' Joshua was standing next to her as she fidgeted nervously with her glove.

Abigail glanced around her; fleetingly she looked in the direction of Biddy's Bakery nervously, before staring back at him. 'I think we would have more time and privacy on our way to Ebton. Don't you think that would be best?'

'If it pleases you, then we shall journey and discuss your problems en-route. Are you sure you wish to damage your reputation in this manner?'

'Sir, I have run away from home, from a marriage, and discovered myself to be of ignoble birth. How much more damaged can I be?'

'The fact that you have asked such a question shows you have no idea of the world, Abigail. I thought it was Molly who I needed to help but it is, I see, you.' He grimaced as his leg ached.

'We shall find transport and be on our way tomorrow. Tonight we must rest. Let's go back to the inn up there and find rooms.'

Joshua was right. Abigail had to admit she had acted out of an irrational desire to find her mother, coupled with the shock that Martha had hidden the truth from her. All those years they could have been together, her and Grace her blood mother, yet Martha and her father had lied to her denying her the truth. The woman had kept so much from her over the years. Abigail would rather take her chances on her own, with Joshua, than with a constant deceiver. As if he sensed her dilemma, he said softly, 'Don't worry, I will keep you safe, but you must trust me.'

They entered the inn. It was busy, as a coach had just arrived. 'Wait here by the door and I will see what I can book for us.'

Abigail was extremely nervous. She followed Joshua to the counter. 'Have you any rooms free?' he asked.

'Might have one,' the man said without looking up.

Joshua hesitated but there was another traveller making his way to the counter. Abigail tapped Joshua's shoulder, he glanced down at her. 'Take it.'

Joshua nodded, 'I'll take it.'

'I need a room,' the traveller said.

'You best try The Angel over the bridge. My last one just went to the gent and his Mrs.'

The traveller turned and stormed out.

Joshua took the key, 'Come, my dear, our room awaits.' He picked up both bags and limped up the narrow stairs whilst Abigail discovered where the room was.

It was only as the door was shut behind her and she was staring at a double bed that she realised what she had done.

★ ★ ★

'Martha, calm yerself. You'll be having a fit if yer don't stop fussing about the lass.' Biddy slammed the dough down on the board in front of her.

'You don't understand, Biddy, she's a lady . . . innocent. Whatever will I do? I'll have to go after her. She can't cope on her own, she's . . .'

'With a gentleman and a damn good one at that!' Molly's remark made Biddy laugh and Martha turned to face her, quite stunned by her words.

'Is he? Is he, though? Or is he just a man looking for a victim — first you a young lass, now he has moved on to a lady. You tell me. For I don't know what to believe, and you don't either. Glad you found your voice, lass.'

Molly looked up at her. 'He is a good

man. I know that. He'll fight for a woman so you've nought to fear.'

Biddy laughed. 'Well, girl, if he fought for you he sure should fight for a 'lady'.'

'That was uncalled for!' Martha said.

Biddy was about to reply but shrugged.

Martha sighed, she knew Biddy was relieved that now there was only her and the girl. Two sets of extra hands to help.

Martha was shaking with rage and guilt. 'Biddy, whatever am I to do? Abigail is innocent of life and now she's roaming the countryside. What have I done to her? I should have told her the truth of it.' She paced up and down the small room.

Molly put an arm around Martha's shoulder stopping her mid-pace. Biddy couldn't contain her thoughts. 'Martha, you sort yersel' out, woman. You've done everything for that babe. You could have had a life and babes of your own if you hadn't given your every waking minute to bringing her up. Face it, she's a spoilt child. No, there's no use protesting, that's what she is! She's never wanted for anything . . . ' Biddy insisted.

'Except a mother of her own.' Martha snivelled, and leaned against Molly for a moment.

'Oh, me heart bleeds for her.' Biddy turned around placing her two chubby fists on her ample hips. 'Look at what she's had instead — <u>you</u>, yer soft 'aporth.' Biddy laughed softly and shook her head at Martha. 'Look at this slip of a lass. Don't yer think she'd have been a lady if she'd been in your 'lady's' boots? No, don't fret for your Abigail, look at the likes of this chit of a girl and weep for them if you must, but not one dressed in silks. If that madam has a lesson to learn in life you let her learn it now, then she'll treat you with a lot more respect in future.' Biddy slammed a lump of dough onto the counter and started to knead it with both fists.

'You don't understand what happened, Biddy. There's so much she could find out that I don't think I'll ever see her again.'

'Well then, let your worldly gentleman show her.' Biddy's laugh was coarse.

Martha pulled herself away from Molly's hug. She ran out of the room and up the stairs to the bedchamber. Pulling on her coat, muffler and bonnet she stormed back down the stairs, through the bakery to the shop.

'Where do you think you're going?' Biddy asked her.

'To do what I should have done a long time ago, to tell her the truth, all of it, Lord Hammond cannot touch me now.' Martha turned to Molly. 'And you, my girl, need a damn good wash, you smell!' She stormed out into a darkening street.

'Charming, just when I was warming to her!' Molly said.

'Follow her and see which way she's off. I'll shut up shop here, then you come back and tell me where she's gone and we'll bring the old fool back. I don't know, as if she ain't lost enough already. He made her give up her life for that bairn.' Biddy wiped the flour from her hands and shook her head, grey hair escaping her cloth cap. 'Go on, lass, quick like.'

Molly walked up the street, keeping to the side wherever she could.

'Good, we'll be better off looking together.' Martha's voice made her jump slightly as the girl turned to see Martha smiling warmly at her. She had waited on the corner for Molly to follow her.

'Did you mean what you said, Ma?' Molly asked, and looked quite seriously at her new friend.

'What about telling her the truth?' Martha asked.

'No, about me stinking?' Molly said quietly.

'Yes — well a bit.' Martha grinned at the young woman's offended face, 'But who doesn't?' she added as if to soften the offence.

'Your precious Abigail, I suppose.'

Martha gave Molly a stern look but it

was met with an equally defiant glare. Martha saw Biddy appear with her coat flapping loosely over her dress as she strode up the street towards them. 'Bloody hell, we've got a search party going.'

'Now you've closed me shop up and will no doubt eat me out of house and home, where do you think you're going next, Martha?' Biddy huffed and puffed as she had walked briskly up the steep street.

'I can't just leave her, Biddy. I love her like me own daughter.' Martha looked at her relative.

'Soft as . . . ' Biddy shook her head at Martha. 'Look around you. What do you see?'

'Houses, both old and new, inns, ships, boats, building yards and people. What am I supposed to be seeing?' Martha asked.

'That's right, and a darkening sky. There is no way that they have left the town today. They're holed up somewhere.'

Martha looked around her. The sky was looking bleak as it cast its shadow of the old abbey on high. The Swing Bridge crossing the Esk that divided the town into two halves, closed shut after a ship had passed through.

'But night time's approaching and she's with a man,' Martha whispered.

'That's as maybe but we just can't ransack every yard and boat in the area. You'll have to believe the lass here that the man is honourable. She made her choice, Martha.'

★ ★ ★

Frederick looked at Jeremy across his father's walnut desk.

'Are you sure, sir?' His voice was amazingly quiet and calm, shocked by his own inability to comprehend how Abigail had slipped out of the estate so easily, then manifest herself in York and apparently travelled to London, yet had not been booked on the coach. No one of her description had been seen. No chaises had gone to London and no gigs hired.

'Then she is still in York. That is obvious,' Frederick concluded.

'If she is, there's word out on the streets that I am looking for her and a reward will be forthcoming, yet we hear nothing, Frederick. She has to eat. The maid has to buy them food. Someone at some time will see one of them and soon.' Jeremy Hackman was determined, and his frustrated manner adamant.

Frederick looked at his companion. He knew the man wanted Abigail in every way. He could not wait to have himself a young fertile wife of, if not breeding, then status, and with Frederick's blessing and his father's money, Abigail fitted the man's preferences to perfection. He was a man who did not like being outwitted, nor defeated. Frederick admired and loathed him equally, but that was how Frederick viewed most people. His mother had been the only pleasant exception and now she was no more than a fading memory, except for her portrait in the grand hall, to remind him of her good looks.

'So we sit and wait, but if no one has sighted either of them within forty-eight hours, then we cast our net wider, my friend. The woman, Napp, is resourceful and Abigail has a certain amount of intelligence ill befitting to her sex.' Frederick flicked a letter opener in his fingers thoughtfully. 'So when is the next shipment due in?'

'Friday. Oberon sent word it will be big and we should have everyone ready. They're getting a bit touchy at present. Gossip sayin' that there is going to be another attempt at closing the ring down.' Hackman poured himself another brandy and sat down on the chair opposite.

'Then tell everyone to take extra care and, if there are any loose tongues around, silence them.' Frederick leaned back and folded his arms as he gazed at his father's bookshelf. There was a gap where the Bible had been. 'I wonder,' he said. 'Excuse me, I think I need to check on my father. I'll be back shortly.'

Frederick went up to Abigail's bedchamber and searched for the Bible. It was not there. Why take a heavy Bible with her when she was trying to get away so quickly? There had to be a reason and the person who knew what that reason was would tell him. He clenched his fists and sighed. Why could his father have not been happy with him alone? He had an heir, what need did the man have for a girl. That he would never understand.

11

Joshua placed the bags down on the carpet by the end of the bed. There was a warm fire burning in the hearth and a small window which let in a dusky glimmer of sunlight. The room smelt musty. The bed itself was soft, covered by heavy blankets.

There was no other furniture save a washstand upon which had been placed a water filled jug in a large chipped bowl.

'Cosy,' he said, and smiled.

Abigail swallowed. 'I didn't think . . . I'll have to go back and sleep on a chair at the bakery tonight and we can leave in the morning.'

He walked over to her, placed her hand in his and sat down on the bed. She saw him grimace as he took the weight off his leg.

'Listen, Abigail. Your reputation has

been damaged already. You are not going to be comfy in a chair in a bakery and I don't think your spirits are sufficiently raised to face Martha again. So tell me what it is that drove you to such a rash act.'

'I found a note she had hidden from me. It was from my father, or the man who I have called Father for my life. It said Mother lives in Ebton. That is north of here. I must go and find her. It also said I was to be kept away from Lady Fenton-Grange, but I don't know why. Will you take me to Ebton tomorrow?'

He was thoughtful for a moment. 'There may be a good reason for you not knowing your mother. She may have wished it so.'

Abigail refused to believe that. It was not right. For some reason the lady had been kept from her. 'I am prepared to face that, if it is so, and I shall apologize to Martha if that is the case.'

He nodded. 'Very well.'

'What is wrong with your leg?'

'I had a bullet removed some months ago and I am still convalescing. It is nothing to worry about.'

Abigail saw a tinge of sadness in his eyes and realised that he was convalescing from more than just the wound. 'You are in no hurry to return to the war?'

'I have not been given the option to.' He ran his fingers through his hair. 'I am, in a sense, killing time instead of an enemy, whilst I recover. I should be lying in some bed somewhere counting sheep. I believe that I need to strengthen my limbs again and I can only do that by using them. I will take you to Ebton, and we shall see what it is that they have hidden from you.'

Abigail could not help herself. She had wanted to know her mother all of her life — one she believed was dead. She felt so happy, she flung her arms around Joshua and hugged him. He wrapped his arms around her and she nestled in to him. It felt the most natural thing to do, but then he kissed her lips tenderly. She did not think, she responded to his touch. She found herself returning his kiss with growing inner yearning. They leaned back and toppled onto the bed. Even as she lay there, she did not allow a single thought inside her head to distract her. He leaned over her, stroked her cheek and kissed her again, more urgently but he was neither rough nor intrusive. He was almost laying over her. It was only as he lifted his head away from hers, propped himself up on one elbow, pausing to look at her, that she felt a flush of shame. He kissed her quickly on her lips and rolled off her, standing by the side of the bed.

'That was unexpected, Miss Abigail, but delightful.'

She sat up. 'I am quite ashamed, I . . .'

'Don't be,' he said. 'You are your own woman now. You are a beautiful woman and I will not apologise for following my heart, but only for upsetting yours, if I did.'

'No, you did nothing to distress me.' She walked over to him. 'I am a fool, Joshua. Martha called me one and now it is proved. I am a fool who is behaving shamelessly.'

He wrapped his arms around her and held her close. 'Tonight we share the bed. You sleep under the covers and I shall sleep fully clothed atop them. Then I might be able to sleep and will not do your honour any more damage. For, Abigail, I ask you to trust me when I am not sure if I trust myself.'

★ ★ ★

Frederick opened the door to his father's bedchamber. He walked briskly across to the bed and saw the sunken features of what had once been a strong, determined and ambitious man. He looked pitiful and broken by life.

'Wake up, Father, I think you have something to tell me.' Frederick waited a few seconds but Lord Hammond slept on. Without compassion he shook the slumbering man's shoulder; the man's bones could be felt through his nightshift. 'Oh, we are in a bad way, aren't we?' Frederick muttered as his father moaned.

'Father!' Frederick shouted, 'Father! I wish to speak with you. Tell me, what was in your Bible? The one that Abigail took with her. Where did she go?' He was not getting any response, so changed his approach. He knelt beside the bed and placed a hand over his father's. 'Listen to me, Father. I am wracked with concern. Can't you see that I am worried about her? Her reputation will lie in ruins if word of this should become public gossip. Please, tell me where it is you sent her, she may be in mortal danger.' Frederick tried to sound desperate and genuine as he thought it was the only way he would reach his father's laudanum drugged mind. However, all attempts failed. 'What am I paying the physician for? Damn it, he's the best man in York and still you waste away! If you die on me I'll have his reputation for his bungling ineptitude!'

Frederick turned around and kicked out in a fit of temper. He knocked the bedside table over with his hand as he stormed out of the room, slamming the door shut behind him. He did not see his father's eyes open, the strain that left the man's expression, or the final smile that crossed his face knowing he could slip away in peace because Abigail had escaped Frederick's selfish and embittered grip.

★ ★ ★

Martha awoke, whilst Molly slumbered on three quarters of the bed. Martha deliberately rolled off the edge that she had been gradually pushed towards through the night and dressed herself quickly. She grabbed her bonnet. Her hand reached for the door handle as she glanced back at the sleeping figure of her new friend. The lass looked like she had fallen from hell and landed in a feather bed of heaven. Martha ran down the rickety stairs and straight into the bakery. Two girls had already been baking through the early hours of the morning. The shop was ready for opening and Biddy was just coming in through the doorway with her shawl wrapped tightly around her against the strong morning wind.

Martha was tying her bonnet in place upon her head.

'Now, just you stay where you are, Martha.' Biddy stood directly in front of her.

'I've got to find her. She's been gone a whole night, Biddy! He could've . . . he could've . . . ' Martha swallowed as she was trying to control herself but she almost shook with her distress.

'What do you think he's done? Tupped her? Murdered her? Or escaped with her?' Biddy asked, without any sound of tangible emotion in her voice at all.

Martha was disgusted with her sister-in-law's response to her Abigail's plight. 'Don't you talk about Miss Abigail in that way. She's a lady!'

'Oh, stop yer blithering, woman. She wouldn't be the first 'lady' to fall for a handsome sailor now would she?' Biddy linked Martha's arm and walked her back into her little parlour away from the ears of the two girls who worked away diligently.

'Sailor?' Martha queried quietly.

Once the door was closed and they were out of earshot Biddy whispered, 'Do yer want those two gossiping all round Whitby? Think, woman, before you go letting off your mouth. She's on her way out of town right now as we speak. Happy as a lark she was when I saw her get up next to her gentleman friend.'

'Gentleman?' Martha asked.

'Yes, if I was twenty still, well maybe thirty years younger, I'd have tupped him mesel'.' The woman laughed loudly.

'Biddy!' Martha snapped.

'Oh, where's your humour woman?

She doesn't deserve you, you know. Your gentleman seems a good sort like your little friend said. Let it be, Martha. She's made her bed and knows where you are if she needs you. There's no way I can get you safely to Ebton so stay here and wait till the bairn comes home. It's what we women do, remember. Besides, he could be the making or the breaking of her. Time'll tell.'

Martha looked at her and all the unshed tears of the years without her man, deprived of her husband and then her other love, Ezekiel, flowed out and she collapsed in Biddy's ample arms. Martha was comforted for once, like the child.

The door opened slowly as Molly's sleepy figure emerged. She stretched and yawned then saw the state of Martha, and Biddy hugging her. 'Bloody hell, what's happening now?' the girl asked, and was greeted by the full force of one of Biddy's 'looks'. Molly shrank back, then smiled and said, 'I'll get us all a nice warm drink, eh!' She closed the door behind her, quickly retreating to the safety of the bakery.

*   *   *

With the moors on their left and the rugged cliff tops and bays to the right, Abigail and Joshua set off on what looked to be little more than a well used track. This was the road to Ebton.

'This isn't as good as the York road, is it?' Abigail commented, as she looked around at a group of motley looking sheep that were idly ambling across their way ahead.

'This is a remote part of the country, and I have chosen to take a route which is not the main coach route, but we should be able to travel some way along it unseen and undisturbed.'

*   *   *

Molly ran out of the back of the bakery. Martha had cajoled Molly into going with her when they had to fetch some fresh vegetables for Biddy.

'I thought I was waiting for Christmas to come, lass,' Martha said, and shook her head as Molly finally left the warmth of the bakery.

'I was just . . . ' Molly started to explain.

'Aye, helping yourself to some off-cuts no doubt. Take care young'un, children have been hung for less,' Martha said anxiously, and then linked her arm with the girl's as they walked down the narrow back alley together.

'Biddy's fine, I help her out you know. I'm not hanging around here for charity. I'll keep on 'til sundown if needs be. After all, I'm used to working the night hours, aren't I?' The humour left her voice and Martha stopped her in her tracks and was about to rebuke her for dwelling on the past, when Molly smiled brightly and added, 'She's all bark and no bite, that Biddy.'

'Lass, there's no flies on you, is there?' Martha laughed at the carefree nature of the youngster who had become so much a part of her life in such a short time. It was as though two lonely souls had somehow found each other.

'I should think not . . . I washed you know.' Molly pretended to be indignant.

'I know, I've been sleeping with you and I'm mighty glad that you did.' Martha's smile dropped as it so frequently did these days as she became pensive once more. She should have been sharing the room with Miss Abigail.

'She'll be fine. He's a good man, a real gentleman. He'll keep her safe, you see if he doesn't, Ma.' Molly squeezed Martha's shoulder as they walked along.

'Do you fancy him, Molly?' Martha asked quietly.

Molly's usual joviality left her as she turned to Martha and said honestly, 'What's the good of someone like me liking someone like him? He's quality merchandise, older and wiser, and I'm poor goods, know nowt, Ma.' Molly shrugged her shoulders and looked at the ground.

'Oh, lass. He may not be right for you, but don't run yourself down like that. I tell you straight, you is pretty as a picture — when you wash up, and brush that wild hair of yours. There's many a man would be glad of a good woman like you.' She stopped and made Molly look straight at her. 'There's no fault in being a victim of life, except for accepting that that's all there is when you've been given a better chance. You live your life and keep that chin up in the air, you hear me?'

Molly flung both arms around Martha and squeezed her tightly. 'You're marvellous, Ma, I love you!' She placed a smacker of a kiss on Martha's cheek and bounced off down the street leaving Martha both stunned and speechless.

She couldn't ever remember Abigail doing that with so much feeling in the whole of her life. This girl loved her for whom and what she was, without looking down, up or sideways at her position.

'Come on, Ma,' Molly shouted back to her.

Martha smiled broadly and caught up with Molly, linking arms again as they happily went about their business.

'That's the inn where they stayed last night.'

'All night!' Martha repeated. She could not help herself worry, sickened by the thought of what they might have been doing, or what he could have done to her. Her Abigail, no better than a, than a . . . Molly turned to look at her and Martha felt ashamed, for hadn't she just been telling this girl to hold her head high. She couldn't help herself, though, she had wanted so much more for her Abigail. It was only right that she helped to give her the life her mother had had to forego, to make up for what happened to her dear friend, Miss Grace.

'Martha, snap out of it, you look all

maudlin' again. Let's get this veg and get the hell out of here whilst we still can.' Molly led Martha down the alley and out into a courtyard.

Both women scurried off as fast as they could to the market, avoiding the main street and nipping in and out of cuttings, which Martha suspected Molly was used to doing all over York. Martha was gasping for breath by the time they returned to the bakery but Molly looked as if she was enjoying every moment of their adventure.

'She's well puffed, Biddy. Had too many of your lovely pies,' Molly said, as they entered the bakery together, laughing.

★ ★ ★

Frederick entered the room where his father had been seen by the physician and consequently declared dead.

The new Lord Hammond stood by the large bed and stared down at the body. Tears streamed down his face. 'I

213

was never enough for you, was I?' he said to the motionless figure. 'Well, I'm the Lord now and the brat is where she belongs — hiding in the gutter. Goodbye, Father!'

He walked out of the room without looking back.

★　★　★

Joshua took them on a road that by-passed the main workings of the alum factories. There was a village there to house the mine-workers. Abigail was shocked at the state of the people because they and their homes were so poor.

'I don't like this place, Joshua, can we go faster?' Abigail was relieved when they speeded up.

'It stinks,' Joshua admitted.

'They should have better conditions.' Guilt filled her as she realised that Lord Hammond was half owner of the works and therefore responsible for the state of it. It was so far removed from her own life that it did not seem possible that two such different worlds co-existed side by side: one providing luxury for the other. 'It's a very lengthy process. The alum has to be mined, boiled and separated from the mater liquor. It takes a very long time,' Abigail said, and was pleased to see the impressed look on Joshua's face.

'Did your father teach you this?' Joshua asked her.

'I asked him what alum was and he explained the process to me,' Abigail reflected. 'I listened to him, you see.'

'Hold on tightly.' Joshua picked up speed. With some urgency they made their way across the headland and round the bays until they approached the fishing village of Ebton, nestled beyond a rugged headland in the curve of a sweeping bay.

Abigail held on tightly to Joshua's arm as they made the descent into the bay. Yorkshire cobles, the flat-bottomed fishing vessels, were lined up on the soft sandy beach near the road. Abigail felt both great joy at the prospect of finding her mother again and sadness at the thought that Joshua would leave her here.

'Abigail, what is your mother's name? I shall make inquiries as to her whereabouts at the store.' Joshua looked at her inquiringly; his eyes seemed to have lost their sparkle. Abigail wondered if he too felt the same mixed emotions as her.

'Grace,' Abigail answered with enthusiasm.

'Grace what?' Joshua asked obviously humoured by her vague and inadequate answer.

'I don't know that,' Abigail admitted quietly, as Joshua's smile faded and he looked upwards, shaking his head in dismay.

⋆ ⋆ ⋆

The old part of Ebton comprised of a group of fishermen's cottages nestled along the sandy bay, behind which the town was beginning to grow. The headland framed what had once been a village, sweeping down with sand dunes covered by wild marram grass. Abigail saw a windmill in the distance, and the spire of a Norman church. More modern terraced houses were being built on the higher land at the back of the town, and a wooded gill took the eye up towards the coast road and to the moors beyond. It was wild, beautiful and as moody as the sea itself. As they entered Ebton they were looked upon with a wariness that made it obvious instantly that visitors did not come to this place often. They passed by a small inn. It looked as though it was built onto the beach itself. All along the shore Yorkshire cobles were lined up on the flat sandy beach. Crab pots and nets adorned the stretches of beach in between. This was a working town, but somewhere within it was, Abigail hoped, her mother. She was filled with a sense of panic. What if she turned out to be a fisherwoman? Would it matter to her? Abigail knew it shouldn't but her own life had been far removed from such a place as this.

'I almost cringe at the thought of asking this question, but Abigail, have you any idea where your mother is living or 'if' she is still living.' Joshua stopped the gig; they braced themselves against the wind which swept in over the sea. Although he spoke to her, his attention was taken by the headland. He seemed lost in thought as he stared back at the raging sea, watching the relentless pounding it gave the rocks.

'We could try the inn?' she offered as a suggestion.

He let out a sigh, looked at her for a moment then smiled. 'Excellent idea, I should have thought of it myself.'

They entered a building that looked like a small inn. A tall man, smartly dressed, greeted them. 'Good morning, sir. Can I help you?'

'Yes, thank you for asking. Few people around here are disposed to look at us, let alone speak or offer help,'

Joshua answered frankly.

The man laughed. There was a warmth to the man's nature that Abigail sensed. 'You are strangers to these parts, which automatically makes you something to be wary of. Who is it you are looking for, sir?'

'Actually, it's a lady called Grace,' Abigail answered, as Joshua glanced down at her, a little lost as to what to say.

The man looked at her, stopping what he was doing instantly. 'And what would you be wanting a lady called Grace for?' he asked.

'I may be related to her,' Abigail answered honestly, as his eyes studied her carefully, to widen as he came nearer to her. Previously, he had paid more attention to Joshua.

'What is Grace's surname, miss?' he asked, staring at her from only three feet away. He was even taller than Joshua.

'That I do not know, sir. Do you think you can help me to locate her? It's important . . . Please?' Abigail could barely hide the sense of desperation and frustration that she was feeling inside.

He did not answer at first. 'How old are you, miss?'

'That is an odd and personal question, sir,' Abigail replied, not wanting to admit the truth in front of Joshua and this stranger.

'Perhaps so, but if you are wanting me to help you find Grace then I would strongly suggest that you tell me honestly.' He folded his arms and waited for her reply.

'I am nearly one and twenty,' Abigail said, and saw the look on Joshua's face showed a fleeting glimpse of surprise. She had led him to believe she was two years older, but could not hide the truth now. At last it had to be told.

The man sat down on one of the rickety chairs. His eyes stared beyond them. At first Joshua and Abigail both looked at each other, wondering if he was in shock or something, but then they turned and saw the figure of a woman, leaning against the doorway. Her hand was placed against her stomach as she stared intently back. Abigail could not prevent her mouth from dropping open, for it was like staring into a looking glass that returned an image of herself, some twenty years older.

'Grace?' Abigail asked. She walked slowly towards the woman.

The woman's trembling hand covered her mouth. For a moment Abigail thought she would turn and run from her.

'Don't go, please,' she pleaded. 'I mean you no harm, I just wanted to meet you and find out who you are . . . if you really are my mother.'

Grace was obviously shocked, as Abigail had instinctively guessed correctly about whom she was and what she had been thinking of doing. The lady stood straight, composing herself. Abigail could see what Martha had meant when she said it had been a name that fitted her bearing well.

'I do not know what to call you . . . miss.' Her voice was shaky, but had the air of gentility about it.

'Abigail.'

Grace's lip almost trembled. 'My mother's name!' she said, struggling to control the emotions that were clearly baffling her senses as she stared at Abigail.

'Martha Napp has been my lifelong maidservant; you know her I believe,' Abigail added and noted the change in her mother's countenance as the name was spoken.

The woman's face hardened. It was as though a cloud shadowed it at the mention of Martha. 'She kept you for herself!' the woman said bitterly and with an incredulous tone in her voice.

As if walking in a dream Grace came over to Abigail and gently stroked her cheek with her delicate hand. A tear ran down her face and Abigail did not know whether to laugh or cry with her. 'It really is you — my baby, all grown up. Able . . . look, my child, it did not die, they lied to me!' She stared into Abigail's eyes. 'She didn't die. All these years she lived and I never knew.' Then the tears fell free, no longer controlled as they escaped. Both women hugged each other for all their years lost.

Able put a hand on Joshua's shoulder and led him outside. 'They need some time.' He looked at Joshua. 'Come with me and I'll make you a drink. They'll join us when they're good and ready.'

Able took Joshua inside the back room of the inn. 'So tell me, sir, where has that babe been all these years?'

'I will be glad to if you could tell me what really happened the night a mother was told her child had been lost to her and a lord took in an orphan.'

Able nodded and both listened to the other with great interest.

Abigail stared at her mother, who appeared to be caught somewhere between total shock and pure joy. She hugged her one minute then sat back as if she had acted improperly, but then gave in to the irresistible urge to hug her again.

'I feel like I know you, yet at the

same time you are a stranger to me.' She cupped Abigail's face in her hands and stared at her through moist, pale green eyes.

'Abigail, that is such a pretty name, and like my mother it suits you,' she said quietly.

'What would you have called me . . . Mother?' Abigail asked, and felt a lump rise in her throat as she swallowed back her emotions.

''Mother', I like the sound of that. I would have called you Lizzie, after the old queen, Elizabeth. She was strong and clever, but I think it is better that you are your own person and have your own name. It really suits you well.' She placed her hands delicately in her lap as she sat down on one of the chairs. 'Did Martha Napp choose your name for you?'

'No, my father did. They told me I was rescued from a life at the alms houses after being found in the abbey grounds by him, and Martha was employed as my nurse, then maid. But that's not true either, is it? None of the stories I was told were. Until I departed from Beckton, with my maid, I had believed that I was from the almshouses. Frederick believed me to have been found in the grounds of Whitby Abbey, so he must have had more knowledge of what really happened than I. It is most probable that, rather than being found there, I was taken there after being separated from you.' Abigail watched as her mother stared at her in disbelief.

'Child, who is this man you call your father?' There was a sobriety about her voice that surprised Abigail.

'Lord Hammond,' Abigail answered, and watched the other woman's face pale once more.

'Edmund, Lord Hammond?' she asked, gripping Abigail's arm firmly. 'He had you all these years?' She stood up and paced up and down, anger filled her being.

Abigail nodded not understanding the weight of the words she had spoken.

Grace hugged her sides and bent over, sobbing uncontrollably. Abigail wished with all her heart she could remove the years of pain, replacing them with ones of pure joy.

'You know my father?' Abigail asked, although the answer was apparently yes.

Grace straightened her back and wiped away her tears. 'I'm sorry, Abigail. You did not come all this way to find me, just to see a gibbering wreck. However, this has all been quite a shock.' She forced herself to smile, and Abigail saw a flicker of life in her mother's eyes that filled her heart with hope that they would be united in their joy, but it would take time to heal the years apart.

'Yes, I knew Edmund, but not as well as I believed I did. We have a lot to talk about, my dear Abigail. Let us join the men and have a warm drink to calm our nerves before we discuss matters further. It looks as though Edmund has kept much from both of us. I pray one day that I shall be able to forgive him his cruel deception.'

Abigail stood up and was led by the hand, like a child, out of the inn and into the room at the back where Joshua and Able were sitting talking in a friendly manner, by a warm and comforting fire.

'You must forgive my manners, sir. I have not properly introduced myself to you.' Grace smiled at Joshua and offered him her hand.

Joshua stood up, offering the chair he had been sitting on to Grace.

'Nor I you, but under the circumstances, ma'am, that is perfectly understandable.' He smiled warmly at her. 'Allow me to introduce myself. I am Captain Joshua Rusk, your daughter's chaperone for this journey.'

'He is a gentleman, mother,' Abigail added.

Grace smiled warmly at him then side-glanced at Abigail, almost as if she sensed the close bond that had built up between her and Joshua.

'I am pleased to meet you.' Grace

looked at Abigail. 'My dear child,' she sighed and smiled as if she was at last feeling the love held within those words, 'I shall introduce myself properly to you. I, dear Abigail, am Miss Grace Hammond, your adopted father's youngest sister.'

Abigail swayed slightly. Her head felt strange. She looked at Joshua but he moved sideways, then at Able; his strong features seemed blurred. She tried to focus on the beautiful face of her own mother who was also falling, then blackness came as she lost all consciousness and fell into Joshua's arms.

★ ★ ★

Martha and Molly returned to the bakery as the light faded from the sky. Biddy was waiting for them. She'd been drinking and was sitting in the chair by the open fire.

'So yer decided to come back at last. Scaring me to death yer were.' She hiccupped then belched loudly.

'I think we'd better get her to bed, Ma,' Molly said, looking tired and strained herself.

'This is more than we needed.' Martha and Molly together took her through to her room.

'Come on, Biddy. Get yerself to sleep and have some sweet dreams for all of us,' Martha said, as they tucked her in.

'Sweet nightmares more like it,' Molly muttered, and received a gentle clip on her head from Martha. Then they returned to lock up the shop door and stood at the bottom of the rickety wooden stairs side by side, neither placing a foot upon the step.

'She's always been one for a drink, 'as Biddy.' Martha shook her head. 'That's why I didn't expect to find her still 'ere when I came back after all these years.'

'You go in first, Ma,' Molly said, and smiled nervously when Martha glared at her. 'I'll make sure no one follows us.'

'Say a prayer, girl.'

'Dunno how,' Molly answered, and

shrugged her shoulders.

'Well now's a good time to learn!' Martha linked arms with the girl and started ascending the steps to the room door. Martha struggled with her superstitious nature, and tried to remember what young Abigail had said to her in the coach about it.

'Our Father, who art in heaven . . .' She paused, and stared at Molly who was straining to remember the words, then she repeated them after Martha as they entered the dark room.

Martha sat on the chair. 'Amen. I've kept such secrets, Molly. Abigail will hate me when she finds out the truth.'

'Whatever you kept from her, Martha, you did it for her own sake.' She smiled warmly at her friend and tilted her head on one side. 'So what is it that's so terrible a secret anyway? Tell me, Ma.'

'She was never 'found' in the abbey grounds, nor taken to the alms houses. No babe would survive those temperatures on a Hallows eve. No, it was where Lord Edmund had told me to fetch the babe after Lady Isabella Fenton Grange had told me to 'lose it'.' Molly stared vacantly into the room as if seeing all the ghosts of yesteryear haunting her, shadows of wrong.

'Lose it?' Molly repeated, her face contorted at the thought and the implication of the words.

'Aye, lose it. She's a bad 'un that bitch is, for sure.'

'So how did Lord Hammond get involved with it?' Molly asked.

'A year or so earlier Lord Hammond found a place for his runaway young sister as governess to Lord Fenton-Grange's son, Georgie. The man was a business partner of Lord Hammond and a good friend. Anyhow, Grace, Abigail's mother, had refused her parents' choice of husband. They threatened her with all sorts of punishments and hardships if she did not agree to the match they had chosen but she wouldn't have it. She had a strong will. In the end she decided to run away. She, like Abigail, had no knowledge of the world outside Beckton Manor, so she told her brother, Edmund, who she loved and trusted equally, and was always close to, of her plans. He had a wife and a boy of his own; he was a good man in those days. So he helped her. Her father had said he would cast her off, throw her to the streets if she refused the marriage one more time. He would have, too. He was a real brute of a man. I think that's where Frederick gets it from.' Martha shook her head.

'So what happened to change it all?' Molly asked, obviously fascinated by the whole story.

'Two things happened within a year of each other. Firstly, Lady Georgiana died giving birth to their stillborn daughter, then Lord Hammond learned that his beautiful, innocent Grace was about to give birth to Lord Fenton-Grange's bastard.' Martha placed her head in her hands. 'Such a beautiful, loving creature, ruined.'

'How on earth did he hear about

that?' Molly asked wide-eyed.

'I told him. I knew that Lady Isabella was barren and bitter, that they had no heir. Georgie had died of the pox and Lord Fenton-Grange had taken advantage of poor Grace. Lady Isabella had told her they would look after her and the baby and see them right. What Grace didn't know was that, if the child was a girl, it would be 'lost' and who knows what would have happened to Grace? — disgraced, penniless and wanton. If Abigail had been a boy then it may well have been legally adopted, or at least recognised in some way. It was too horrible to think about, so I helped her to get a message to her dear Edmund. But he, too, had changed. He'd become a dishonourable and bitter man himself. He had sought to improve the fortunes of his estate by ill dealings with the likes of Hackman and Drab. He grieved for his wife and had dearly wanted their daughter. Instead of rescuing his fallen sister and her child, he saved them, but at a price. I was sworn to help him keep them apart. Only I knew the truth of it, but he threatened me, Molly. I'd nothing, no man, no bairns, the only roof I could hide under was this'un and it had a brood of it's own to cope with. The only way I could protect both was to stay with Abigail, as he ordered me, and let Grace live her life out in relative comfort and ignorance in the small town of Ebton. Fenton-Grange swore to Edmund that he had been warmed by drink and that his sister had flirted with him mercilessly. He had succumbed to her as Adam to Eve. Both men had invested interests in their 'business' so it was agreed no more would be said on the matter. She was taken from Dower House with the least fuss, provided with a nurse and housed in the only place in Ebton where there was a half respectable room for her to live in comfort — the inn — until she was strong.' Martha put a hand on Molly's shoulder.

'What would have happened to her if

his lordship had just taken the babe?' Molly asked.

'God only knows, but a woman with no means and in a weakened state doesn't survive long, as well you know, Molly. Each year she has been paid an adequate allowance, but Edmund told her most severely never to darken his doorstep again, and she never did, not knowing that the reason was because he had stolen her child to replace his own. It was of his blood and he convinced himself he was being charitable. You see, he reasoned that Grace had acted slovenly and selfishly when she could have been cosily wed, so, making it all her own fault. Funny, isn't it, how people can work things round to suit themselves. Only the boy, Frederick, was a jealous little brat, who hated her on sight. He covered it well enough, and Abigail was very like her ma. She never realised until his lordship fell ill and Frederick moved back to claim his inheritance. Even he did not know that in fact he was hating his own cousin.'

Martha looked down on the face of Molly. 'Compared to you, lass, they've all been blessed, to what your life has been, eh girl?' Martha stroked the girl's head. 'But I still did my friend a grievous wrong, even if the right of it was well beyond my power to influence.'

'You saw them both safe. What more could she or anyone have expected of you? Never mind, Ma, we've got each other now. I reckon we've both got a bit of living to do.' Molly hugged her tightly.

Martha patted the girl's back. She'd always wanted a girl of her own. Could it be possible that she had found one, someone who could be as her own family? She stopped thinking for a moment and sniffed the air.

'Now, don't you go getting all maudlin' again, Ma,' Molly said, and looked at her worried face.

'No, lass, I'm not, but I can smell burnin'.' Martha opened the bedchamber door but the smoke was already filling up the stairs. They slammed the door shut and opened the window opposite.

'Bloody 'ell, Ma. We'll have to shimmie down onto the lower roof and shout for help.' Molly was pulling Martha towards the window.

'I've got to help Biddy,' Martha shouted.

'Then get yourself out that window whilst we still can,' Molly shouted at her and pushed her over to it.

'You go first, rouse us some help. It'll take me longer to get down. I ain't nimble anymore. Oh, poor Biddy, what's to be done?' Martha almost shoved Molly out of the opening.

Before Molly left, she turned back to Martha. 'Promise me you'll come too, Ma, you're all I have.'

'I promise,' Martha replied, and the girl left as smoke started to seep into the room.

★　★　★

Abigail awoke some hours later in a pretty little room with very feminine trimmings surrounding her; the quilted cover that enveloped her had such delicate tiny stitches that she thought the person who had made it must have had great dedication to her task and took great pride in her work. It must have been a labour of love. Everything seemed to have been carefully made and matched and the warm hues made her smile. It was as if the interior of the room belonged to a far grander home than a humble cottage. She was filled with such a peculiar sensation as she looked at the lady sitting upright, reading a book in the chair next to her bed. It was, she realised, an overwhelming sensation of love.

Grace smiled at her and stroked her brow. Her eyes were filled with concern for Abigail's well being. 'Do you feel better now?' Grace asked gently.

'Yes, I'm sorry for . . . I can't think what came over me. I am not given to such fainting fits.' Abigail tried to sit up but her mother placed a gentle hand on her arm.

'Please, Abbie, stay. Rest here for a while.'

'I must tell Joshua, that I am well. I can't imagine what he must be thinking of me.' Abigail slid her arm from under the delicate hand and sat up.

'Your young man has left you in my good care as he has had pressing business that he needed to attend to urgently. He asked me to give you his deepest and sincerest apologies and to convey a promise that he would return to you as soon as he could.' Grace patted Abigail's hand as she looked shaken by the news.

Had Joshua been so eager to rid himself of her that he could not wait for her to regain consciousness? It was as if her thoughts had been read by the older lady as she spoke.

'And I don't think you need worry about what the young man thinks of you, dear. He looks totally besotted and I can well see why, but he appears to be a man with a mission, so let him see to it in peace. I am sure he will return to you as soon as he is able.' Her smile was warm and reassuring.

'But we have not known each other very long and such things have happened in such a relatively short time,' Abigail said the word and both women smiled. They had accepted each other and shared in the same joy.

'I know, Abigail, sometimes friendships happen that way. Only others can interfere, which is why I have asked Able to watch over him.' Grace winked at her and Abigail realised her mother was both a resourceful and an astute lady. She cleared her throat in a nervous gesture.

'Able is my dearest friend. I owe him my life and my happiness. He is a very special person to me, Abigail. I hope you can accept him as that, as I do.' She waited for Abigail's response.

'How can I but respect the man who has looked after you so well all these years. Are you happy here, though,

Mother? The people seem so distant and cold,' Abigail added politely. 'Perhaps you could return to Beckton. Father is very ill. I'm sure after all these years old wounds heal. Perhaps you could help him. I think Joshua may have gone there to find out what has been happening. He wouldn't betray us, though, I'm certain.' Abigail stared at her hopefully but she saw hardness replace the gentleness in her eyes.

'How can my wounds regarding Edmund have had time to heal when I have only just learned of his predetermined deceit? I can not do that, I lost your lifetime — your childhood, seeing you grow into this fine woman — all lost to us. I was thrown out of that place and I never wish to return to it. How could I cast my eyes upon Edmund again? He hid you from me; your whole life I have believed you to be dead. I have lived with the guilt for the last twenty years, thinking I was not strong enough to save you, that I was not there for you when you needed me to be. No, I am sorry if he is unwell, I would not wish ill upon him but I shall not make one step towards him. A reunion is out of the question, and if that son of his wants the whole pile to himself then let him have it. It has brought nothing but pain to generations of Hammonds, why should it change now?' Grace patted her hand. 'I'm sorry to speak to you in such a way.'

Abigail held her mother's hand. 'What are we expected to do then, just wait here?'

'It's what women are supposed to do, isn't it?' Grace answered pointedly, but with a glint in her eye.

'So we sit and wait?' Abigail asked with a sickening feeling of inadequacy lurking within her.

'Of course not!' Grace replied, and Abigail watched her stand up straight. She was graceful but there was strength about her that Abigail sensed and admired.

'Tonight we sleep like babes. Tomorrow, we return to Whitby, and you can take me to see your 'maid'. It is time I said hello to Martha Napp once more.' She opened the room door then glanced back at Abigail. 'Stay there. I shall fetch you something to eat, then we shall sleep as mother and daughter, together at last.'

Abigail watched her go and was overwhelmed by the sense of pride she felt. She had prayed that she would not find the shell of a once proud woman, but Grace was far from a shell. She was her own person, and Abigail had made her feel complete, as she herself would have felt if only Joshua were still there with them. What on earth would Martha say when she turned up with her mother, Grace? She chuckled to herself at the thought; they would soon find out. Then, she thought, let Martha dare to tell them both another lie!

*   *   *

The flames licked the front of the bakery so that no one could enter.

Water was brought up from the harbour and pumped onto the burning building. The laundry women helped as much as they could and all effort went in to saving the houses next to the bakery, lest the whole town burn.

Molly was staring at the back of the bakery and shouting hysterically, 'Martha! Martha!' Some fishermen caught hold of her and dragged her away. The girl started screaming uncontrollably in her distress. She couldn't see what was happening. Tears stung her face as she thought of her idyllic future crumbling, or burning to ashes, before her eyes. Suddenly, a bag was flung over the yard wall and Molly recognised it as Martha's. She grabbed it quickly as a hardly recognisable bundle of smoke-stained rags was carried out between two burly men.

They put her down on the ground and Martha animatedly coughed and cursed.

'Martha, you're alive!' Molly hugged her and the woman cursed even more at the turn of events.

'Are yer hurt, Ma?' Molly asked, trying to control herself and gulp back her tears.

'Of course I'm bloody hurt! I slipped off the roof and landed on those two ugly brutes. Nearly broke me neck, I did. I told you my days of shimmying are gone. Where's that Biddy? I couldn't get back down the stairs. They'd folded before I could set foot on the bloody things.'

'You mean you actually tried? Oh, Ma, you could've died.' Molly hugged her tightly.

'Well I didn't and I gave you me word. Now, gerroff me and stop fussing lass. I've got to find Biddy.' Martha sat up and rubbed her eyes, trying to stare through the darkness of the night at the gathering crowd.

'Dunno, Ma. No one could get into the front. Everyone tried, but it was no good.' Molly looked at the face of Martha as she waited for the reaction to her words, their meaning slowly sinking in.

Martha stared at her for a moment. 'Oh, Molly, what have I done? I knew that bad things would happen if I returned to this God forsaken place. I tell you it's cursed, and me with it.' Martha grabbed Molly's hand and pulled herself upright. The girl picked up her bag.

'Take me around the front, I need to be there when the flames die down and they bring poor Biddy out.' Martha looked at Molly through watery eyes. She saw the sheer relief in the girl's face that she at least lived, but the overwhelming guilt that Martha felt for Biddy, engulfed her whole being.

Molly nodded and they walked around to the front. The fire had been turned and the building could be saved, although the shop was gutted. The flames needed to die out completely, though. No one would enter until morning at the earliest.

They stood there, staring as the crowd started to disperse.

'Where do we go now?' Molly asked.

'An inn tonight, then tomorrow, who knows?' Martha leaned her head against Molly. 'Oh lass, I'm so tired of it all. Just when summut goes right, all hell breaks loose and all's lost again.'

'Fine bloody mess this is!' declared a loud voice from behind them.

'I know, but what can we do now?' Martha answered it, but Molly glanced back, standing speechless with her mouth hanging wide open.

'Nowt, that's as plain as can be, but you've let the bloody place burn down. Can't a woman go and get herself a well earned drink without her house being torched whilst she's not there?' Martha and Molly looked at Biddy as she swayed behind them and then sank to her haunches as she held her head in her hands, still drunk but still very much alive. 'It's a nightmare — I'll wake up in a minute and it'll be all peace again.' She swayed back and fore holding her head and muttering to herself, occasionally taking a swig from a bottle in her hand.

They laughed with relief and cried at the same time, but all Biddy could do was moan, repeating one phrase, 'Bloody hell! Bloody hell! Bloody . . . ' She rolled back too far and lost her balance, falling onto the wet ground, where she stayed staring up at the stars.

Molly and Martha had tears of joy overflowing, but as it started to rain heavily, dousing the embers still further, they struggled to get the large figure of Biddy upright.

'Come on, woman. Tonight you go to an inn. We'll sort out the mess tomorrow.'

They manoeuvred her to her feet and hooked arms with her.

'It'll be alright, you'll see, Biddy,' Molly said brightly to her. 'See, you've got us.'

Biddy's ruddy face swung around and faced young Molly, it swayed like her body. 'Bloody hell!' she repeated.

★ ★ ★

Early the next morning Abigail found Grace by a small leather travel case. She heard Abigail enter the room and welcomed her warmly. Abigail had dressed but not had time to arrange her hair, which looked decidedly in need of a brush.

'Good morning, Abbie. I hope you slept well.' Her manner was charming and bright.

'Very well, and you?' It seemed strange to Abigail that she had slept with a total stranger who was her own mother and yet it had felt so very right. 'It's still dark,' Abigail said and yawned.

'No, I didn't sleep at all well, but that was because I was so happy and excited by yesterday's events. I felt as though I should wake myself up out of this dream, a dream I have had so many times, then awoken to realise I was alone, my baby gone,' she gave Abigail a hug, 'but in fact this dream turned out to be real and, yes, it is still dark.' Grace put her arm around Abigail's shoulders and sat her down by a cup of hot milk, a board on which had been sliced some freshly baked bread, and a pewter plate on which were delicately arranged pieces of ham and cheese. 'It is the early bird that catches the worm and we have a short chubby one to catch today, Abbie. So move yourself along a bit, then I'll dress your hair and we can be on our way. I've left a letter for Able, in case they return before we do.'

'He can read?' Abigail asked, and then looked at her mother a little nervously in case she had spoken out of turn. 'I mean, I would not expect many of the people in Ebton to be able to.'

'It's all right, Abbie, I'm not offended and neither would Able be. Yes, I taught him how to. He is a very clever man and never tires of learning new and challenging things. Now hurry up with that, whilst I fetch our bonnets and coats. Abigail, I hope you don't mind but I took a few things out of your bag and placed them in mine. I thought we may need to stay overnight.' Grace looked at her quite worried.

'That's fine, Mother. I don't have anything to hide from you.' Abigail thought that at last she had found someone who she could trust with her whole heart. Unlike, it appears, her father, who was really her uncle, although she hoped he had recovered and that she would be able to persuade her mother to change her mind and see him again. Whatever wrong he had done, it would be her dearest dream if she could somehow see brother and sister reunited.

'Good, unlike Edmund, you can trust me, Abigail. Now we are together, let us keep it that way. It makes life so much more simple and enjoyable. Now, eat up.' Grace smiled at her and Abigail ate heartily.

All hope of a reunion drifted from Abigail's mind as she ate the fresh food. The hurt was too deep in her mother, and Abigail had to accept that her dearest dream was not to be. He had grievously wronged her and that was a new pain Grace and Abigail would have to come to terms with, but this time they would face their future together, burying the past.

'Are you angry with Martha or relieved she looked after me?' Abigail asked as she washed up her plate.

'We'll see. I will know for sure once I see her face again. She has kept you from me knowingly. She knew I lived here and yet she left me thinking you were dead. I have taken flowers to the church for you regularly. At one time I thought of joining you.' She looked ashamed at her own thoughts.

'Thank God you didn't, or we would never have been together anywhere,' Abigail said, as her mother brushed out her hair and arranged it with her bonnet placed neatly on her head.

'Well, I didn't and I am so glad of that fact now. My dear, we will walk towards the coast road and stop at Downing's. If he has a chaise available I'll pay for us to travel to Whitby in some comfort, otherwise we will have to wait for the stagecoach.'

Within minutes they were headed towards Downing's suppliers to the local gentry of chaises and quality horses.

'Will it be open at this hour?' Abigail asked, as the sun rose in the sky over a calm sea.

'Oh yes, people here are hard working, Abigail. They start early and go to bed late. Tell me, has Martha been a maid to you throughout your life?' Grace glanced down at her.

'Yes, I've never been without her, until I came here to find you, with Joshua.' Abigail admired the straight posture of her mother as she walked along, head held high, back straight and a natural grace to her step.

'Then why would she not come here with you as a chaperone?' Grace asked, 'Or was she in fear of seeing me again?'

'I didn't give her the chance. I walked out on her and asked Joshua to chaperone me. He is a gentleman, Mother,' Abigail added defensively.

'No, he is not. It is in no way fitting

for a young lady to be travelling such country with him on her own.' Grace was firm in her manner, but not unkind.

'Some might say the same regarding your reputation, and your friendship with Able,' Abigail spoke directly hoping she would not offend.

Grace stopped and turned Abigail to face her. 'Abigail, I lost my position and reputation many years ago. I have been living as an outcast to 'polite' society and to these people for nearly all my life. Is that how you would choose to live?'

'I was brought up in a gilded cage, surrounded by possessions and two people whom I thought I knew, whom I believed in, and thought I could trust, but they lied to me for twenty years. They both knew I had a mother and yet they kept you from me. I never knew who, or what I was, except I discovered recently how much my presence was hated by Frederick, for being a bastard. Would I like to live here? Yes, if I could be with my real mother.' Abigail spoke from the heart and with total conviction.

Grace wrapped an arm around Abigail and hugged her to her. 'We have both been wronged, but let us be on our way and we shall try to sort out this mess.'

She strode off at a pace, and Abigail followed carrying the small case. Grace seemed to have even more determination in her stride as she approached the iron gates with 'Downing's Yard' written within their workings over them.

'Now, smile and be pleasant. Remember you have no need to cower to anyone, you are a lady, born and bred,' Grace reassured her.

Grace's face glowed with genuine pride. Abigail silently watched her mother negotiate a fair price for the chaise. Within minutes they were on their way once more, back to Whitby, where her story began.

Abigail had mixed emotions about seeing the distant Abbey once more.

She felt guilty at walking out on Martha and was not sure how much bitterness her mother felt towards her old friend. The chaise pulled up by the harbour bridge. The driver helped her mother alight, then her, and handed their baggage down. Grace gave the driver a tip. Then, as he pulled away, she turned and breathed in deeply. The air was bracing. Fishing boats had already set sail and the boat yards were noisy and busy.

'It's been a long time, Abbie. It brings back so many mixed emotions to me.' She linked arms with Abigail.

'The bakery is down here. I left Martha with her sister-in-law . . . ' Abigail started to explain.

'You mean Biddy is still here?' Grace asked, obviously surprised like Martha that she still ran her business.

'Why, yes.' Abigail and Grace cut through the snicket by the inn and stared in horror as they were faced with the remnants of a burned out gutted bakery.

Abigail ran across the street. 'Martha!' she said out loud. She turned to face Grace. 'Mother, I left them here. Oh, dear God, what have I done? She can't be . . . ' Tears overwhelmed her. She had been so blinded by her own anger that she had given no thought to their future. But now, faced with the ashes, not knowing if Martha's ashes were mixed with the remnants of those of the building, she felt empty and sick. Martha had always been there, with her, throughout everything. Abigail realised she expected she still would be.

Grace put a comforting arm around her. 'We'll find out what happened and if she is alive, injured or dead.' Her voice was steady, matter of fact and strangely without emotion.

Abigail wiped her eyes on her sleeve. 'Sorry, yes, you're right. I mustn't jump to conclusions.'

They turned to walk up to the coaching inn. There they would be able to find out the whole truth of what had happened, and if there had been any survivors. Abigail looked up. 'Molly!' she shouted to the girl who was walking down the street towards them. 'You're safe. Tell me, is Martha safe? Does she live? Did she escape?' Abigail ran the few feet to the young girl, who once again looked grubby after the night's events.

'Why? Do you care or are you scared that your servant will no longer be fit to do your bidding, eh?' Molly's voice was filled with bitter resentment. Abigail was quite taken aback. She was aware that Grace had moved up to the side of her.

'Of course I care, she's my Martha, I . . .'

'No, she ain't! She don't belong to you. She belongs to herself. She is Martha Napp and deserves to have a life of her own.' Molly stared at Grace. 'Is this your Ma then?'

'I am Abigail's mother, yes. Who are you?' Grace asked politely.

'I is Molly, and she don't need Martha no more, as she has at last got a ma of her own. You go and leave Martha with me. I'll take care of her, so bugger off before you gets her all upset and maudlin again.' Molly's face was flushed, her anger obvious but she looked tired and drawn.

Grace grinned widely, which seemed to annoy Molly and surprise Abigail. But whilst Abigail had had her eyes fixed firmly on Molly and her reprimands, Grace had seen the familiar figure walk down the street behind Molly.

'Listen, lass. I've never needed anyone to fight my corner and I don't intend to start accepting it now.' Martha put her arm around Molly's waist.

Martha looked at Grace, and Abigail saw her mother's eyes water.

'You seem to have a knack of surviving, Martha,' Grace said gently.

Molly scowled at Abigail, who stared defiantly back at the girl. Her words had hurt her deeply, mainly because of the power of truth that they carried.

Martha opened her mouth to speak to Grace, but her bottom lip trembled as, simultaneously, they stretched out their arms and hugged one another.

Molly looked at Abigail accusingly. 'See I told you, she'd get all maudlin again!'

★   ★   ★

'We cannot stay here and freeze, ladies,' Grace said brightly and Abigail saw Molly raise her eyebrow slightly when they were all referred to as 'ladies'.

Martha stared at the pair of them. 'I'd like it if you two could be friends. You are both a part of my life, past and present, so please try to be at peace with each other.' Grace nodded her approval of Martha's words.

Abigail smiled broadly at Martha and adopted her mother's tone. 'I'm sure we shall.'

Molly smiled sweetly, and replied with her best attempt at polite speech, 'You bet we will, just like real sisters, eh?'

Grace looked at Martha and said, 'So let us find somewhere warm and private where we can discuss the future.'

Martha nodded, and all four women turned as a voice exploded behind them. 'Bloody hell, me business is gone, me life's in ruins and you all stand 'ere gossiping. What the hell are we going to do now?'

'Have a cup of coffee, I think,' said Grace, and patted Biddy on the back.

The fat woman chuckled. 'Bloody hell, you're like a damn phoenix, did you spring up from the ashes themselves?' she addressed Grace.

'No, but I like the analogy,' Grace replied and ignored the confused look on Molly's face as she spoke.

'Aye, I'd need a lot more than a cuppa to get over this reunion. Come and help me see if I've got owt worth saving first.' She headed over to the bakery.

Biddy and Molly carefully tiptoed inside the building. Martha and Abigail stepped forwards but Grace put her hand out on each of their arms. 'Two's enough. Biddy, we shall be in the hotel, we have things to discuss.'

Biddy's reply was muffled and unclear, but the expletives were easy to pick up.

'We'll see you there when you're ready,' Grace shouted and walked off.

Abigail and Martha followed, unusually ill at ease in each other's company.

'I'm sorry I walked out on you, Martha. It was a stupid thing to do.' Abigail saw Martha smile.

'I'm glad you realised it, without any harm coming to you. So what have you done with your gentleman?' Martha looked at her.

'He had business to attend to,' Grace explained.

Grace was standing tall, staring down the street at the side of the hotel. A yellow and black coach was parked alongside the building, the driver waiting, ready to go.

Martha saw what she was staring at. 'Now, lass, don't go getting any ideas Grace. Bygones an' all . . .'

'Abigail, we shall acquire a table. You must wait for Biddy and the young girl, whilst Martha and I say hello to an old 'friend'.' Grace faced Martha who was looking decidedly unsure.

'No, Grace, it will do no good,' Martha pleaded.

'Yes, Martha, it will. You owe me, woman!' Grace's voice was firm. They entered the hotel, Martha was extremely nervous, Grace, however, was strangely calm and Abigail looked most concerned.

'Mother, let me come too; this concerns me doesn't it?' Abigail asked.

Grace looked at Abigail thoughtfully for a moment. 'Yes, it does.'

A hotel boy in a smart jacket came up to Grace. 'Can I help you, ma'am?'

Grace's demeanour became all charm and elegance. 'Yes, you can.' She produced a coin. 'Lady Fenton-Grange was kind enough to lend me her carriage. Can you give the driver a message?' The boy, seeing the coin, nodded eagerly. 'Can you tell him the lady said that she has finished with him and her maid for the day? They are to go back to Dower House and return in the morning for her. Mind, not too early though.' The boy held out his hand for the coin. 'Can you remember that word for word?' she asked.

'Yes, ma'am,' he said keenly.

'Repeat it, word for word,' Grace insisted.

He did and the coin was his. They sat at a window table and watched as the driver received his orders, and the maid inside the coach complained bitterly. However, the driver somewhat reluctantly pulled himself up onto his seat and drove off.

Martha looked at Grace who smiled broadly at Abigail. She admired the calm manner in which her mother behaved. 'Now what?' she asked.

'We have coffee,' Grace said, as she watched the door to the back rooms of the hotel.

Lady Fenton-Grange appeared from the back room of the hotel and walked boldly out to her carriage, shocked that it was not there. She turned to re-enter the hotel and was faced with Abigail, who smiled charmingly at her.

'You again!' she snapped. 'Tell me, girl, where do I know you from?'

'You've met her once, I believe . . . as a baby.' Grace's voice made the lady turn her head slowly towards her.

'You! You can't be. You didn't survive, neither of you did.' She started to back away and, before she realised where she was, she found herself in the middle of the road, by the harbour side.

Martha rushed forwards. 'You be careful now, Lady, you could trip.'

She ran to the other side of the cobbled street. The ground was slimy and slippery. Some people stared at her, as she was known for her aloof appearance and her fancy coach. No one had ever seen her look less than perfect, in dress and composure. But now, with mud spattered skirts from a passing wagon, hair buffeted by the strong wind, she didn't look so grand. The three women crossed the road, but she did not want to be near them.

Grace spoke first as the woman inched away from them. 'This woman is the one that you would have had murdered at birth, Lady Isabella. Indirectly, granted, you would have sent her weak to the poor house and no doubt they would have seen to her for you. I want you to see what you did with your meddling. We are united at last and you have nothing but your money and your drunken buffoon of a lord for company. He raped me and how many others? Tell me, does he still live or has he caught some disease from you?'

'Leave me alone! I'll call the dragoons!' she threatened, as Grace approached her.

'I have no wish to harm you, woman. I just wanted you to say sorry for the years of hurt you caused us. Then your soul may not rot in hell's fire for eternity!' Her voice stressed the last few words.

Isabella took one last step backwards to turn and run away, but her delicate shoe slipped on the salty wet slabs and she tripped over a discarded coiled up rope. Her beautiful silk and wool cloak and her skirts absorbed the mud and moisture making it difficult for her to stand up quickly. Isabella began screaming and kicking out like a child in mid-fit. Martha slapped the woman's face hard to bring her back to her senses, whilst Abigail and Grace linked an arm under each of hers and helped her to her feet. Her kid gloves were muddied and ruined. She sobbed, ruining her made up face.

'Come, you are not worth the bitterness of revenge. I forgive you, and leave your judgement to God.' Grace looked at the other two. 'We shall book her a basic room at the inn until her coach returns for her in the morning.'

'In the morning!' Isabella shrieked, clearly distressed at the thought.

'Yes, you shall have a night to yourself to contemplate your misdeeds.'

The lady was, for once, at a loss for words.

★ ★ ★

Joshua and Able entered Whitby down the steep incline of Baxtergate as Isabella was being led back into the hotel.

Abigail's face lit up as she saw him, and Grace smiled broadly at Able with undisclosed joy that he too was safe.

Both men looked exhausted by their ride. Joshua dismounted, his appearance unclean and dishevelled. With a clear bruise on his cheek he looked a figure far removed from the gentleman who had accompanied Molly into the same town days before. He came straight to Abigail's side.

'I told you to stay safely in Ebton,' he said, and was obviously finding the temptation to reach out and touch her very strong. 'Abigail, I'm afraid your . . . 'father' died,' he said tenderly.

Grace squeezed her hand and Abigail looked down, but somehow she had come to terms with his loss, as gradually her image of the man she had

268

loved as her father had been shattered. 'My uncle, as it turns out,' she said thoughtfully. 'Now Frederick will have everything, as he wanted to all along.'

'I'm afraid not,' Joshua answered. 'His joy will be short lived as some of his and his father's deeds have not been exactly legal. He shall be arrested soon enough.'

'Abigail being here is my doing, sir. We had unfinished business to attend to in Whitby,' Grace explained.

Joshua stared at the lady who was propped up between them. She peered into Joshua's face.

'Well, look what the tide's brought in.' Molly was plainly pleased to see Joshua again. Her skirt was covered with smudges from where she had been helping Biddy find her money that had been hidden under the floor in a secure box. Fortunately, the stone slab on top of it had protected it from being burned too.

'What happened here?' Joshua asked.

'The bakery burned down.' Biddy looked thoughtful. 'Oh well, time to do summut else. Like have a cup of coffee or best brew.' She patted her box and went inside the hotel.

'What am I going to do with you?' Joshua looked at Molly, and grinned.

'You don't have to worry about that.' Martha looked at Molly. 'I want to go back to Ezekiel and he could do with all the help he can get at the inn. I reckon we'd both be more than welcome there.' She winked at Molly who smiled broadly.

Molly hugged Martha and Abigail felt a tinge of guilt and jealousy, just for a second, until her eyes focussed on Joshua again.

'What are you going to do, sir?' Abigail asked, with more than a hopeful glint in her eye. However, Joshua looked troubled.

Martha turned Molly round on the spot. 'Come on, lass.' She was frog-marched into the building before she could say another word, leaving Joshua and Abigail standing outside.

Joshua smiled at her, but both their

eyes turned towards the abbey on the cliff.

They walked side by side up the steep bank, climbing the ninety-nine steps, past St Mary's church to the overgrown abbey stones.

There, sheltered from the wind and in the seclusion of the once great house of God, they embraced each other openly and honestly.

'So, Frederick is to be arrested,' Abigail said flatly.

'He has lost everything. He and Hackman will both be arrested. Your mother may yet be able to return to the family estate, should she wish to.'

He stroked her cheek with his hand gently, and she nestled her face into his warmth. She kissed his lips tenderly.

It was Joshua who pulled away.

He looked somewhat embarrassed. 'I have nightmares, Abigail, I have scars beyond those on my thigh. Now, I have become involved with you, entangled in your life and touched by your fate, but you have a mother to discover and twenty years to catch up on.' He hugged her close to him.

'You have helped when help was needed and you have always acted with honour.' She smiled impishly at him. 'Let us spoil you. You need rest — let us make sure you do. Don't rush back to the war or London. Heal. There is no shame in needing to heal.'

'Not always,' he answered honestly, a flush of colour warming his cheeks.

'But consider my own plight, sir. My own reputation lies in ruins.' She glanced around them as she looked at the abbey; the irony was not lost on her.

'Neither you nor your reputation will be ruined; you have a home, a loving mother and a respectable gentleman friend — let us walk out together or limp as is more appropriate? Let me restore your reputation honourably.'

⋆ ⋆ ⋆

'I want to say yes, but I hardly know anything about you.'

'We have all the time in the world to find out. Help me heal. I have a property in London, you will not want for anything again, certainly not love. Stay with your mother, I shall recover then you can both come to the city and see it for yourselves. I have no family left to me other than distant cousins,' Joshua answered solemnly.

She looked into his eyes as he held her close. 'You are indeed an honourable man.'

'Definitely,' he said, and bent over kissing her passionately on her lips. She responded. Despite the cold air around them, he warmed her heart and soul.

★ ★ ★

Mustering her willpower, she turned her head away and breathed deeply almost tasting the fresh salty air.

'Then let us rediscover the people we are and both heal, before we make any further promises or commitments,' she replied.

A broad smile of approval greeted her words. Abigail's heart and head were at once in full agreement. She had no more doubts as to who she was. Abigail had released her past, embraced her present and held on tightly to a very promising future.

THE END